Love in the Shadows

Mariah Lynne

ISBN: 979-8-88653-445-0

Published by Satin Romance
An Imprint of Melange Books, LLC
White Bear Lake, MN 55110
www.satinromance.com

Published in the United States of America.

Cover Design by Caroline Andrus

To the love of my life, my husband Jerry.

CHAPTER
ONE

raced inside the Naples Florida Public Library hoping to avoid a sudden afternoon shower. Once inside, I closed my umbrella and looked around. It's been a couple of years since I was here last, but everything looked and smelled the same. I was just about to take my wet raincoat off, when I spotted an older woman pointing her finger and shaking it directly at me as she hurriedly approached. She came so close that her finger almost poked my eye, and I had to take a couple of steps back. Still shaking that finger in my face, she spoke in the angriest of tones.

"You have some nerve, Lana Brighton, coming back to this your former library to promote a book you claim you wrote about your personal love story. Ha! What could a librarian, especially you, possibly know about love and romance? I remember how you ignored my wonderful son who told me you declined his invitation for a lunch date. You broke his heart, something I'll never forget. Let's face it, Lana, you are as boring as an old spinster who is much too shy to even talk to a man about a book never mind a date. I'll bet you probably have never been kissed because that nose of yours is always buried in some volume. But you don't fool me, Missy, with any of your author claims about romance. I intend to sit close to the front for your talk, to call you out as a liar and a cheat, and to boo!"

With that the irate woman stopped pointing her finger, turned, and huffed off to find her seat in the meeting room. I stood there speechless still needing to take off my wet raincoat.

A member of the library staff I remembered, Cheryl, rushed out to assist me. As she helped me with my raincoat, she advised, "Don't give that old lady a second thought. That's Mrs. Hertly, a constant troublemaker and complainer. Our adult library monitors must escort her out of whatever meeting she attends because of her rudeness and unnecessary comments. I can see two of them guiding her outside now because I'm sure she has accosted everyone and anyone entering the meeting room for your book presentation. But don't worry, the attendees I've spoken with are all anxious to hear about your book."

I smiled. "Thanks for the pep talk. You know, come to think of it, I do remember her son, Stuart Hertly. One afternoon, he grabbed me and tried to kiss me while I was shelving books. Then he had the nerve to ask me to lunch. Of course I turned him down. A bit too aggressive for my taste. Must take after Mom."

"You have no idea how caustic she can be. One of our patrons said she reminded him of a witch and dubbed her The Hag of the Hardcovers since she always hung around the hardcover book aisles and stared at our patrons." We shared a quick laugh over that nickname before I followed her into the meeting room. As soon as I entered, I was overwhelmed to be greeted by a standing ovation from the attendees.

———

As the applause continued, my mind drifted back to two years ago when my unique love story began. As Mrs. Hertly correctly remembered, my name then was Lana Brighton, and on one sunny warm afternoon on my way home from my job at this library, I sensed someone following me. This was not the first time, nor would it be the last. When I turned and blinked, I saw the same shadowy vision of a man I had experienced many times before. His presence was brief, but oddly didn't frighten me, because this shadow had slightly blurry but familiar facial features while his height and build appeared to be the same as a man I hoped to meet again, the man who had rescued me and saved my life after my family's recent fatal car accident. From the moment I met him on that tragic day, I knew I could fall in love with him.

I took my time going home hoping this shadow would reveal himself to me again, but unfortunately, no such luck. I realized I was the only one who could see him because whenever the shadow appeared, passers-by paid no attention to him. When I spotted him in the library, I'd ask "Who's there?" but no one responded. Library patrons who knew about my recent trauma dismissed my odd behavior as lingering psychological problems related to it.

I reached my small apartment building and walked up the front steps alone. My dream hero did not follow. I still couldn't grasp why this shadowy image continued to follow me. Was he a ghost? A spirit? Or a remnant mental effect from my near fatal crash? Did my desire to see this handsome man again seize control of my mind and my imagination?

Once inside, I plopped down on my couch and sighed from my frustration. I glanced at my coffee table but didn't remember leaving the morning newspaper open to the feature section and I sure didn't remember seeing this article about a local Psychic Faire before I left for work.

After all my encounters with this shadowy vision, I needed to find out if he was real or if I was losing my mind, so I confided in my best friend since grade school, Sara. Yesterday, we met for coffee after work, and I asked, "You seem so much calmer and look healthier than the last time we met. How did you cope with those terrible nightmares after your divorce?"

She took a quick sip of her cappuccino. "Lana, I know this will seem unusual especially to a sensible person like you, but I went to the Collier County Psychic Faire last weekend and met with a psychic named Aurellia. Her sign advertises that she helps 'The Most Troubled.' That fit me to a T. She listened to my angst and took care of my problem. Believe me, she helped me understand my nightmares and find my inner peace after my heart-breaking divorce. You know, the Faire continues through this next weekend, maybe you should go and find Aurellia. Give her a chance to explain your visions. I'm walking proof that you can trust her, and she'll do her best to help you."

Knowing how particular Sara was about any kind of service, I agreed to go and find that psychic. I didn't have to work today and was curious as to why I still had these visions. I couldn't let a shadowy figure control my life. I'm better than that, so I decided to seek help from Aurellia to explain who this vision was, if he was real, and if I'd ever encounter him again.

That night, I hardly slept a wink wondering what my meeting with Aurellia would reveal. Determined to find out, I got out of bed early, my stomach filled with those same butter-flies which had plagued me all night. I dressed in a blue and white striped skirt and white silk blouse, and left for the Faire, checking behind me all the way. I blinked and blinked but experienced no sightings. I so wanted him to be real and for us to meet again.

Once there, I scanned the Faire grounds looking at all the tents until I spotted that one sign Sara had mentioned. "Aurellia —Psychic for the Most Troubled." With Sara's advice in mind, I headed straight for that tent. I composed myself and took a deep breath before pushing aside the heavy gold canvas drapes to enter the psychic's tent. I was anxious about what this meeting might reveal.

At this point, I wanted to see that shadowy vision in the flesh so badly, I would have resorted to any kind of help to find him, especially since he haunted my dreams every night. No point second guessing since I was already in her tent. I might as well hear what Aurellia had to say.

The entrance to the main part of the tent was dark except for multiple strings of tiny flashing lights in lavender and rose. Their rhythmic flashes lulled me into a trance-like state, while the fading scent of incense irritated my nose. As I reached into my pocket for a tissue, I also grabbed for my cell phone before proceeding any further. Never having consulted a psychic before, I didn't know what to expect and didn't know if I would have to call for help. Besides, it was dark, and the phone's light would help me see.

I walked further until I saw a light shining between the panels of two emerald- green brocade curtains. I paused to steady my shaking hands before separating them to enter this next part of the psychic's tent with trepidation and hope. Never having done anything like this before, I stopped to ease my pounding heart, wondering if I should continue.

I took a few more steps forward before I stopped again this time surprised by the sight of two beautiful white Russian Wolfhounds. They lay on either side of a small square table covered by a purple lace tablecloth. An elegant-looking woman whom I thought to be Aurellia sat between the dogs. She stood when I entered. The wolfhounds sat up and growled in such a loud and frightening manner, I had to cover my ears. *Were they there to protect her? They looked so fierce, I wondered if I should reconsider my visit.*

"Take it easy, my good, sweet puppies. Everything's all right." The woman's voice made them settle down and wag their tails.

Big babies, I thought, and proceeded.

Aurellia sat with the posture of a queen. I stared into her

kind and inviting deep brown eyes and studied this beautiful olive-skinned woman with waist-length black curly hair. She looked to be in her late forties and dressed like the Romani royalty of Eastern Europe with a rose-colored satin gown beneath a wine-colored brocade and sequined mid-length coat. She smiled and greeted me from her seat at that small square table which held a large glowing crystal ball at its center. "Please, my lovely lady, come sit down next to me."

Her layers of silver bracelets jingled as she motioned for me to come toward her. Her kind dark eyes beckoned me to obey. The more I studied her, I wondered why I even considered taking Sara's advice about coming to this Psychic Faire and if this total stranger would be the right one to help me.

Was my blurry shadow that of the handsome man who saved me? I needed answers since these visions had interrupted my life for the past nine months, making me more anxious to meet him. Finding him would give me inner peace. I shouldn't admit that. I pride myself in being an independent woman. I have a respectable job, my own apartment since I lost my family, and thought I would be able to manage this by myself. I wondered if I should have consulted a doctor or a psychiatrist instead of visiting a psychic. This entire episode may be related to my unusual dreams, but it could be indigestion, my grief, or even stress.

Aurellia sensed my angst at once. She shot me another kind smile and welcomed me again in soft tones. "Please, my lovely lady, come. Come sit down next to me."

I hesitated but Aurellia continued to plead. "Please, my beauty, come. My darling companions Boris and Bohdana will not harm you. Don't fear them. They are big puppies, not yet one year old. Come sit here next to me." She patted the chair next to hers.

I walked over still reluctant to bare my soul to a total stranger and sat on the edge of my designated chair in case I had to bolt out of there. Maybe seeing a psychiatrist was not such a terrible idea. My face flushed. I felt the burn as I jumped up to leave. The psychic gently grabbed my arm and pulled me back down.

"Please stay. If your visit involves a spirit or any unusual visions, tell me about them, about you, and your problem, so I may be of assistance. My name is Aurellia, and I have assisted many over the years with all sorts of psychic problems."

Her intuitive comments startled me enough to sit down and answer her questions.

"Please tell me your name and how I may have the pleasure of helping you. It will be my honor because you could have chosen another psychic."

I nervously cleared my throat before beginning. "My name is Lana Brighton. I am and have been a librarian in the history section of the Naples Florida Public Library for the last five years. I consider myself an independent woman, pay my own bills, and take history classes around my work schedule. I live alone since I lost my entire family in a tragic auto accident nine months ago."

Aurellia's dark eyes remained focused on mine. She leaned forward attentively as I continued. "I adore reading about sixteenth century Europe and will even sneak a read at work. My job requires long hours of silence. There is little or no time for conversation. I'm beginning to think all that solitude may be at the root of my problem, so I discussed my predicament with my best friend, Sara, who suggested I visit the Faire this weekend. She recommended you because you helped her understand her nightmares from her recent divorce and said you would take the best care of me."

Aurellia reached across the small table and touched the top of my hand. Her touch felt so warm and gentle, I didn't pull it away. "I'm glad you're here, Lana. Please tell me more about how you are troubled."

Aurellia's soft voice mesmerized me, but for some unexplainable reason I felt the need to blink. When I did, that handsome shadow appeared before me. I stood and blurted out his presence. "He's here! My shadow's here in your tent!" I pointed to what anyone else would consider thin air. I sat back down in my chair puzzled. "Who is that handsome man...that shadowy figure? Why won't he leave me alone?"

Aurellia turned her head and looked directly at him. When I blinked again, he disappeared. Surprised that she could see him as well, I asked. "What does he want from me? He follows me everywhere."

She touched my shoulder to calm me. "Lana, he's harmless. Pay no attention to him. I will explain later in our visit. Please my lovely lady, go on with your story."

I couldn't believe what she'd just said. I fumbled for words. "Did I hear you right? Pay no attention to him? How can I do that when he *is* the reason I came for help? I see him everywhere, with every blink of my eyes. He's at the library when I put away books. I see him outside my apartment. You just said, 'Pay no attention to him.' Do you know him or anything about him?"

Before I could finish my sentence, I blinked, and my shadow returned. I blurted out. "Do you see him just now? You don't appear to be surprised. On the contrary, you seem so calm."

As soon as he left, Aurellia nodded. "Yes, indeed I did see him. We shall remain the only two who can until his shadowy figure takes human form."

My heart pounded. I was relieved beyond belief that I wasn't crazy but also frightened that this image of a man was real and might harm me. Still in disbelief, I blurted out. "Please Aurellia, tell me again that you saw him, too, and that he is a real person and not a shadow."

Aurellia shot back a kind smile. "Yes, I did see, him and his shadow is one of a real person. As I advised earlier, pay no attention to him for now." Aurellia cleared her throat as if anxious to change the subject. Her gaze zeroed in like a laser on my necklace. "That's an exquisite antique pendant you have on, quite an unusual shape with such a deep colored garnet. I sense it belonged to someone in your family. Am I correct or did you purchase it from an antique dealer?"

Her questions made me forget about that shadow for a few seconds to answer them. "This pendant belonged to my mother who passed it down to me. I'm proud to wear it and proud of its place in my family history. It originally belonged to my ancestral grandmother, Marchesa Genolli, on my mother's side. She was Italian and lived during the sixteenth century in the Venetian Republic. When she was nineteen, she became betrothed to a young Council Member who served as an advisor to The Doge. Marchesa, herself of royal lineage, was a countess, and considered a beauty. The pendant was a gift from her future husband to solidify their engagement.

"When their two families feuded, The Doge cancelled the young couple's engagement and determined Marchesa should keep the pendant since it was a gift. Besides my pendant, Marchesa also passed down a puzzling legend about its value. She claimed its worth was immeasurable, that men would kill for it. That statement has always perplexed me, so I had it appraised. The jeweler said it was worth $1700.00. That's a lot, but hardly an amount worth killing for."

Aurellia's eyes remained fixated on my pendant. Its stones sparkled in the dim candlelight. Aware I had her attention, I continued. "The locket has a three-carat garnet at its center surrounded by tiny diamonds and is set in platinum. Mother told me Venetian jewelers, noted for their artisanship, made the intricate lace-like setting. I love it and am proud to wear it, but I have remained perplexed by its unusual shape. I've always wondered what if anything was inside; that's remained a mystery to me. Perhaps it held a lock of my ancestor's hair or a valuable tiny trinket which once belonged to my ancestor and possesses that immeasurable value she mentioned."

Aurellia asked. "You have never been able to open it?"

"No, and I've been afraid to take it to a jeweler for fear he might damage it. The eldest daughter in each generation since Marchesa has inherited it. When I marry and have a daughter, it will be hers. The pendant has more meaning for me since I lost both my parents and only sister in a head-on collision. It is my only remaining connection to my family."

Aurellia's kind gaze focused on me. "I understand and am sorry for your loss."

I wiped tears from my eyes. "Something odd happened the day of the accident. I was truly fortunate to suffer only minor scratches and bruises but had passed out from stress. I woke up in the ambulance surprised to see a man sitting next to me. Most of the other EMTs were taking care of my family, but he stayed with me. I looked into the kind eyes of a very handsome man dressed in a white shirt similar but not exactly like those worn by the other emergency responders. At that moment, to me, he looked like a Roman god with sculptured black hair that framed his face and strong, chiseled facial features. Since he took care of me, I assumed he was a paramedic. Leaning over the gurney, he had an accent as he whispered in my ear. 'My lovely lady, you are incredibly lucky to be alive. Someone must be watching over you.' After that, everything became blurry, and I passed out."

Since I had just relived the most difficult day of my life, tears formed in my eyes again. Aurellia handed me her embroidered lace handkerchief. Fur as soft as silk rubbed against my ankle followed by a quick lick. I looked down before continuing. Boris must have sensed my angst. He made me smile.

"I came to after a few minutes anxious to see how the rest of my family was, but that proved impossible since a sea of paramedics and flashing red lights continued to surround them.

When I looked for my paramedic, he was gone like he had vanished into thin air. His kind face still haunts me. I think my mind has been playing tricks since the accident to deal with the tragedy. He may have been that good spirit who my mother believed stopped by to escort people to heaven or my mind trying to deceive me, but I did survive and didn't leave for heaven with him. Oh, how I miss my mother." I said, covered my eyes, and started to cry.

"I *am* sorry for your loss and deeply saddened by it. I feel your soul's profound sense of grief. When you are able, Lana, continue to describe your paramedic to me." Aurellia responded squeezing my hand trying to encourage me. Thinking about that kind man made me forget about my grief for a few more minutes.

"Well, to begin with he was very handsome, the handsomest man I've ever met. He had olive skin, light brown eyes like those of a lion, and black curly hair. His smile was magical, calming me the second I saw him. While he was with me, I believed everything was going to be all right. As he adjusted my pillow, I could see how muscular he was. He was polite and spoke using old fashioned terms which at the time struck me as charming."

Aurellia sat back. "Would you like to see him again?"

I laughed, blushing at my response. "Haven't laughed like that in months. Well, honestly, I would," I added coyly. "I can't get him out of my mind."

Aurellia nodded. "That's understandable. Now may I examine your pendant?" I agreed so she reached over and dangled the long platinum chain from her hand. She then held my pendant in the air by its chain to closely examine the gemstones against the flickering candlelight before she pressed it in her hand and closed her eyes. "I sense your ancestor Marchesa knew what secret this locket holds. I also believe her secret will reveal itself to you soon."

I sat back in disbelief as she opened her eyes and continued.

"This is exquisite workmanship. The jeweler selected the garnet for a reason. The garnet is meant to bring a newfound energy to your life. Filled with regeneration, some claim its stabilizing powers will bring order to your life and help you or the loved one you choose to get through the toughest of times. It sounds to me like your life can use these powers. Let the stone's aura and powers take charge so they can go to work for you but remember never to take your pendant off. Always wear it even to bed. There may be others with bad intentions who seek to find what secrets Marchesa's locket holds."

Aurellia gently placed the pendant and its filigree chain back down on my white silk blouse. I stopped crying and composed myself. She faced me with the most intense look. "Lana, it's time to talk about your shadow."

I leaned forward eager to listen and learn. Aurellia spoke in a deep serious tone. "There are many paranormal entities present in our universe. Most remain inconspicuous but others beg for our attention in a constant visible form such as ghosts, spirits, or aliens. Some who only take a temporary visible form are known as Shadow People. Have you heard of such beings?"

I shook my head. "No. I've never heard of such a thing. Of course, I live such a sheltered life, refuse to watch any of those conspiracy channels on the TV, read only history and the classics, and don't have much of a social life outside the library."

Aurellia had stumped me, but I needed to know more. I asked. "You said 'entities?' Yet you classify spirits, aliens, or ghosts separate from these Shadow People as you call them. Is there any correlation between them?" My trained librarian mind tried to make sense of this whole thing by categorizing them.

"Not exactly," Aurellia answered. "Aliens are from another world. Ghosts and spirits have passed on. If you see one, their apparition takes a lasting shape and form like in its former life. Shadow People have not reached that point. They are but a fleeting form in the blink of our eyes. Something or someone is keeping their presence in a state of limbo in our world. They appear as you described as a flash or a shadowy figure across the corner of your eye. Skeptics say they are just a figment of our imagination; some believe they are the precursor to a ghost. Others believe they are Time Travelers who are searching for someone or something from their own time and may assume a temporary human form to complete their quest. Do not be afraid of that shadow. He is stuck in a world that is neither ours nor that of a ghost. Once he gets what he needs, he will leave, and his spirit will pass on to the next world."

I sat back stunned by her answer. "What does he want from me? Am I just to ignore him?"

Aurellia took my trembling hand. "I know this must be difficult for you to hear. We may have to let his visits play out. If you want, we can meet again at my residence. I know the library closes at five so I would be available to see you in the evening. At the very least, don't panic, he will not harm you. He's a lost soul looking for guidance. You must not fear him."

I shrugged my shoulders, finding her advice hard to accept as she handed me her card. "That's easier said than done. I'll call you if the need arises. This may prove too complicated to process alone. I appreciate your time. Thank you for your help."

Aurellia flashed another encouraging smile. "I'll try to contact him on your behalf after the Faire closes tonight. That may be difficult because of the nature of his being. He is not a ghost and may not respond. I may have to reach out to him through a fellow medium named Othero who is more familiar with Shadow People.

"If either one of us makes contact, we'll ask that he identify himself, before asking if he was the EMT who sat with you in the emergency vehicle. If he was, we'd advise him that you want to meet him. Remember there are no guarantees. Call me anytime. My card has my home phone number and address on it. My fee for today is twenty dollars. I'm sure I can be of more help with a longer exchange. The Faire ends tomorrow. If you need me during that time, I will be here."

I nodded as Aurellia shot me a sympathetic smile. I remained tongue tied by her revelations. I had hoped for better news. I studied her reactions again. Could I even trust this woman's judgement and who was this Othero? I took her card, put it in my purse, and paid her fee before adding, "Thank you, Aurellia. I hope you're right."

I stood and left wondering if her intervention would work.

CHAPTER
TWO

My meeting with Aurellia concerned me so much, I had a great deal of trouble falling asleep that night. When I finally did, I dozed fitfully startled awake by every flashing light and creaking noise. As the morning sun streamed through my window, its rays eased my stress. I've always felt strong, and more in control during daylight hours, especially after the horrific dreams that followed my accident. Today, Sunday, I wanted to relax and forget about them.

I got up, began my usual weekend chores like laundry and ironing to help me feel like my pre-accident self. I even got to read without interruption for an entire hour. Sara stopped by around four. As soon as she closed my apartment door, she asked, "Hey girl, did you see Aurellia? She's one savvy lady, isn't she?"

I nodded before she asked. "Did she help you?"

Sara and I were best friends and both twenty-seven. She was attractive with ivory skin, blonde hair, and blue eyes, and ever so smart. That's why I couldn't understand why her husband of four months left her for his assistant. I tried my best to help her through her divorce just like she helped me through my uncontrollable grief after my family's accident.

"I think she might have. It's still a little early to know for sure, but I'll keep you in the loop." I smiled and turned toward the kitchen, "Come on in and get comfortable. I've already started dinner. Homemade tomato soup and grilled cheese sandwiches."

My menu brought a big smile to her face. Comfort food always worked for me. As we ate, I told her about my experience. "Sara, you should have warned me about those enormous dogs. They frightened me at first but turned out to be as cuddly as teddy bears. I told Aurellia everything about that shadow and she assured me she would help. She advised me not to be afraid of him because he means me no harm. I have her card in case I need more advice, and she said I could visit her at her home after work if necessary."

"I'm so glad you went to see her. Please don't be afraid to go back for more help. She sure helped me." Sara replied satisfied with my response.

"Don't worry, I won't be," I answered gulping down my last bit of sandwich. After I picked up the dishes, we left my small kitchen table and went to the couch. "Look at this," Sara said rummaging through my coffee table magazines. "You have all the newest gossip magazines. This is better than the hairdresser. You must have made your supermarket happy."

I laughed. "Yep, I'm sure they were dying to get rid of them. Ah the supermarket, it's the only place I feel comfortable talking to a man I don't know. I haven't had a date in such a long time, I can't even remember when that was. I become excited every time a male bagger asks if he can take my groceries out to my car. It's the only excitement this drab dateless old lady can count on."

Sara was quick to scold. "You are not drab. You're gorgeous. I'd kill for that long wavy red hair and your green eyes. Wow! And old? No way. We're the same age and I don't consider myself old. Those dateless claims of yours fall deaf on my ears.

Remember nice guys are just waiting to meet a beautiful, smart woman like you."

"I will." I responded as we went back to reading entertainment magazines voraciously switching our editions back and forth. What a wonderful day, tasty food, a good friend, fun, and no shadow. Our time together flew by. Sara left around eight p.m. I did the dishes, showered, and went to bed. I lulled myself to sleep with thoughts of my handsome EMT.

Since I must be at work by eight a.m., I'm an early riser. I selected a navy-blue suit, put on my make-up, tied my hair up, and grabbed my reading glasses. I looked into my dresser mirror wondering why that shadow who resembled my EMT chose to stay close to me. No time to think of those things. I snatched my lunch and left for work all the way there wondering if I'd ever meet my handsome shadow in person. Every few steps, I blinked but nothing happened. I didn't see him but did stop short at the sight of something unusual. To my surprise, an adorable kitten raced across my path. Not a black one but a calico one. Good colors since I needed good luck in finding my EMT.

My day, however, did not remain shadowless. As soon as I sat at my desk, I blinked, and his shadow appeared. I gasped. As I did, I blinked again, and he disappeared.

"Lana, are you all right? You're so pale. You look like you've seen a ghost." Mrs. Stith asked.

"Wish I had," I joked trying to compose myself to assist the long line of readers anxious to check out their books. I groaned to myself. *Monday morning shifts are always the busiest and that stupid outburst of mine only made it worse.*

After I found two naval history books for one of my regulars, Captain Reynolds, to peruse, I turned to go back to my desk thinking it's been four hours since my first shadow appearance. That was a terrible way to keep time, but I so wanted to meet him in the flesh. On my way back to my desk for a lunch break, I stopped short and gasped smack dab in the middle of the aisle surprised to see a large book at the center of my desk placed to the right of my computer. *Can't these people read my sign? Returns on the left.*

As I got closer, I noticed the book was open and book-marked to a specific page. I shook my head wondering if I missed helping someone and if they left before I could. Priding myself on being attentive, I looked all around, but no one was nearby.

Curious, I immediately sat to inspect the volume. It was old...very old. I looked at the date of printing...First edition 1588. *Did I read that correctly? 1588? This must be a reproduction.* The more I examined it, the more I didn't think so. The silky pages printed in multicolored inks had large illustrations. Exquisite, they displayed gold gilded edges and embossed lettering. A book of this quality belonged in a museum, not a public library. The book was open to a chapter entitled "The Palace of The Doge." I took a quick peek at the front cover "The Venetian Republic-Volume One-Historical Buildings."

The Palace of the Doge...I was never fortunate enough to visit Venice let alone the palace. Venice has always topped my travel wish list because The Venetian Republic was home to my ancestors. Besides, The Doge of my ancestor Marchesa Genolli's time was the one who allowed her to keep the pendant. I squeezed my pendant thinking about my family history but on a librarian's salary, I'm afraid I will only see Venice in travel or history books. Curious, I turned the book to the inside cover with extreme care. Peculiar, no barcode or catalogue identification number, so it wasn't a library book.

With its pages printed on vellum paper, the book must belong to a collector. I opened the book again to the marked page and was surprised to find a handwritten note. *Why didn't I see this before?*

"This book is a gift for you, Lana. Please take it home and

read about one of the most beautiful buildings in the world." Signed in the most elegant script, "From Someone You Know."

I looked between the shelves again, but everyone had either left for lunch or returned to work. Closing the book, I placed it in my tote bag to read as soon as I got home. One of my regular readers, Mrs. Wright, came to my desk needing help to check out her book shortly after that. Lost in thought, I didn't see her and jumped when I heard her voice.

"Lana? Oops. Sorry dear. I didn't mean to scare you. I just wanted to tell you I saw a man leave a large book on your desk. The book looked quite heavy for a library book. Anyway, he was a very handsome lad at that. Oh, to be your age again. The only men I attract now need bifocals or walkers."

We shared a laugh but in doing so she piqued my curiosity with that last bit of information. Why would a handsome man leave an expensive antique book on my desk? That alone was mysterious and exciting...didn't sound like my life at all. I'll have to call Sara as soon as I get home. It couldn't have been my dream lover's shadow because Mrs. Wright said she saw him. I'm quite sure Aurellia revealed she was the only one besides me who could see him until his shadow took human form. This entire incident made me too nervous to eat my lunch.

I could hardly wait for five o'clock to arrive. I packed the book along with the rest of my things in my bookbag ready to walk home. I took my time carrying the bag up the front steps into my apartment because of its weight. Once inside, I took the large volume out and placed it on my kitchen table. Anxious to read about Venice, I didn't want to waste any time making dinner, so I decided to have my peanut butter and jelly sandwich saved from lunch first with a cup of tea. I washed my hands after eating, hoping to avoid any chance of staining the book's antique pages.

Opening the book to "The Palace of the Doge," I was puzzled why that specific chapter required my attention and if the mysterious gift giver knew anything about my family history. The gorgeous lettering and colorful drawings held my eyes hostage. The illustrations are printed in rich gemstone colors and drawn in detail with gold leaf borders. Since I always dreamed of visiting Venice and the palace, the artwork drew me in like a moth to a flame.

A history addict, I already knew the palace was the seat of power for the Venetian Republic but was amazed at the size and variety of the rooms. Besides serving as the Doge's residence, this large structure also housed grand chambers of government to massive ballrooms fit for royalty and faced the Grand Canal at St. Mark's Square. The exterior entrance to the Doge's private residence was located off a small canal, the Rio dell Canonica, and near the apse of the beautiful St. Mark's Basilica which at one point in history served as the Doge's private chapel.

I sighed as my eyes marveled at the beauty of these illustrations of the old city and the romantic Bridge of Sighs located on that same small canal. I knew the bridge's original purpose was far from romantic even though so many lovers have photographed a kiss with the bridge in the background. I, too, hoped to do that one day.

The bridge's true function was to serve as a walkway for prisoners between the palace's courtroom and jail. It got its name from the sighs of prisoners passing over the enclosed bridge to their cells for what may have been their last day of freedom. I pined nonetheless at its beauty thinking how wonderful it would be to cross under that bridge in a gondola with someone special. With that thought in mind, I put my head on the book, dozed off, and let my imagination do the rest.

I soon dreamt I wore a floor length emerald- green silk gown embellished with a ruffled neckline and train. My shoulders covered by a white fur wrap, I held a colorful hand-painted and sequined mask ready for the Carnival Ball, the biggest social event of the season, a fact that still holds true to this day. Artisans create unique handmade masks for their wealthy patrons. My dream mask possessed a face as beautiful and delicate as a china doll. I imagined a handsome young man also masked and wearing a formal waist coat escorted me to the palace in a shiny black and gold gondola, all the while its gondolier serenaded us.

Once there, my escort led me inside the palace. I scanned the ballroom to see women wearing the most extravagant gowns in all the colors of the rainbow. They surrounded us as their escorts looking regal in their matching formal wear and masks stood by. I dreamt my masked partner swirled me around the ballroom with its Venetian glass chandeliers and walls that held smoked glass mirrors and large works of art until we became dizzy with desire. He held onto me and, looking deep into my eyes, said, "Come my darling. I wish to take you to a place where we can be alone to enjoy what little time we'll share together." He so infatuated me that I followed him out of the ballroom to a private room where he at once removed his mask before he locked the door.

Even in my dreams, I couldn't believe my eyes. It was him! My handsome EMT! He reached for my hands and led me to a gold gilded poster bed where he helped me undress, undoing all the stays on my bodice before he picked me up in his arms and placed me on the soft down mattress. He joined me and as we lay down together, we made passionate love the entire night. As those sensuous thoughts filled my subconscious, I fell into a deeper sleep causing my head to fall off the book and hit my kitchen table. That woke me, making me go to bed.

Those last intense thoughts continued to fill my dreams until my loud alarm clock interrupted them. Six a.m. No more dancing...no more handsome man ...no more love tryst. I must get ready for work. I wondered if my dream meant we would meet today. Happier with that thought, I dressed and packed crackers and cheese for lunch.

I arrived at the library a few minutes late. I was lucky it was not my day to open because patrons were already waiting in line to check out books. There's always a rush first thing in the morning, even on a Tuesday. As soon as I caught up the line, I checked in the returns on my computer. I left my desk when I saw an older gentleman waving me over. He was happy to see me. "Good morning, Lassie, my name is Edwin McBride, and I need help finding a book on Scottish Royals with dates between 1500-1700. I recently discovered that one, the Earl Angus McBride from the late 1600's, may be a relative. I'd love to tell my grandchildren more about him. A colleague at my former employer, Scotland Yard, had a hobby of researching past criminals and advised me that Angus was quite a scoundrel and a thief, even taking bold chances like trying to steal the royal jewels. Trust me, I've met the likes of him many times over when I worked at Scotland Yard. Proud to say I'm retired now. I want my grandchildren to realize being royal does not make you innocent of any crimes."

I smiled. "Finding Angus sounds like fun. What are we waiting for? Let's get started." He followed me to the right section where it took me all of ten minutes to find the perfect history book with all the information he needed. When I opened it to the first page of that story, there was a drawing of what old Angus looked like. "Well, look at this. You have inherited many of his facial features."

I held the page up for Edwin to see. He laughed. "Thank you, Lassie. You helped me find my ancestor, such as he was. My grandchildren will be delighted to see this drawing. I've passed on word-of-mouth stories about him and his misdeeds to them, but now they'll know for certain he was a real person. As I always advised them, 'Family lineage does not make you who you are. You must earn your reputation through hard work and good deeds.' I'd be most grateful if you'd check this out for me after I find a mystery book to read for pleasure."

His comment made me happy. Helping people is what I love about my job. "No problem, sir. I'm delighted to help. When you're ready to check out just come to my desk." With that, I turned to head back to my desk when I bumped into a tall, mustached stranger. Dressed in black pants and a long-sleeved royal blue shirt, he stepped aside bowing to allow me to pass without saying a word.

Odd, I don't remember seeing him before. What's this? When I returned to my desk, I saw a dozen long-stemmed red roses in an ornate black and gold smoked glass vase resting at its center. Puzzled by their sudden appearance, I walked over and peeked at the gold gift card.

"From an enchanted patron to a beautiful lady."

Could that odd mustached man be the enchanted patron? I sure hope not. Before I could finish that thought, "Lana is it your birthday?" became the question of the day. Everyone who passed my desk had a question or a comment about the flowers. I did my best not to be rude, but it was none of their business, especially since I needed time to sort this whole thing out. I know it wasn't the old Scotsman; he wasn't fast enough, but that stranger?

Relieved to leave all the unwanted attention behind, I sprung from my seat when Mrs. Dinter walked up to my desk. "Lana, I need to find photographs of World War Two dresses. I've been invited to the most wonderful event, a military tea party decorated in that era. I was asked to wear a fitting histor-ical dress and of course I want to look my best."

I left my beautiful roses to assist her. Together we found several books and periodicals, with many black and white photos. Mrs. Dinter was so elated she gave me the biggest hug. "You know I think you're the best librarian in the world. You help so many of us. Thank you."

As she perused the photos, I walked back to my desk only to stop short, stunned by another surprise. I uttered my words loud enough so anyone nearby could hear." *Another book...How could this happen?"* Lucky for me, no one was in ear shot.

Another large volume rested to the right of my computer. I hurried over, anxious to see how this volume differed from the first. Its cover and size were identical to the first one. To say I was flabbergasted was an understatement, so I sat down at once to examine the second book. It was titled "Volume Two: The Hidden Treasures of Venice."

Volume Two? I barely had time to read Volume One. Is someone playing tricks on me? Just like Volume One, this large edition was opened to a specific chapter "The Small Treasures of Venice." The page was marked this time by a delicate pink crocheted bookmark, while the chapter summary explained how many small treasures remained hidden in many of the secret passageways and walls of the old buildings including The Doge's Palace. I was very curious to learn more about them but knew I shouldn't read at work. I closed the book and placed it in my tote bag. My roses were so lovely I was disappointed I couldn't take them home as well. The weight and size of this book made it impossible for me to carry both. Still, I remained anxious to read about those small treasures after work.

With no more surprises or gifts, the rest of my workday seemed peaceful. Except for my roses and that newest volume, everything at work remained normal, but a normal day always made me happy. My roses and the new book added another layer of mystery and curiosity to my life in a good way...not like the memories from my accident.

Anxious to read about the treasures, I hurried to complete my afternoon chores and clean up my desk. I glanced at the large wall clock. Five o'clock. I couldn't wait to leave. I added water to my roses hoping to keep them fresh for another day, picked up my bag, and left for home.

I opened the front door to my apartment and closed and locked it with my double bolt security lock. A woman living alone can't be too careful. I walked into my kitchen and placed the book on the table next to the other one. An unnerving sensation came over me like someone was staring at me. I blinked and my handsome shadow looked right into my eyes. I wanted to be with him, but these unannounced sightings made me anxious, made me wonder if something was wrong with my mind. He disappeared as soon as I blinked again.

I took a deep breath, deciding a cup of herbal tea would help calm me. I filled my tea kettle and put it on the stove as my mind continued to work overtime. How could my EMT be a Shadow Person? *Do I even believe Shadow People exist? Aurellia's no doctor. She's a very good showman who probably concocted the entire story for cash. Her Shadow People are no more real than the man in the moon, but to be sure, I'll research Shadow People in the Magic, Mystical, and Psychic section of the library tomorrow after work.*

After a few sips of my tea, I calmed down and ran my fingers over the newest volume's silky maroon cover, its soft cool touch relaxed my mind. I inspected its exterior. It was well kept considering its age. Opening the book to the marked page, I became mesmerized by reading the first article about an ancient treasure missing from a chief advisor's residence since 1538.

I then studied the detailed illustrations of the many large buildings built near the Canal. It was well known that many structures from that era had secret passageways and hidden rooms. I had read about such secret rooms before but not these specific passageways mentioned in the chapter's introduction which had been modified for the storage of valuables in concealed floor boxes elevated over the canals or those placed under the eaves of a roof.

The missing treasure featured in this chapter was a royal crown dating back to thirteenth century Constantinople, minted in eighteen karat gold, and embossed with platinum figures and leaves. The artist's drawing showed two tall, thin religious figures in long robes sitting on high backed thrones; one figure was carved on each side of the crown. Taken as plunder in Constantinople by the Venetian army for the reigning Doge of that period, this spoil of war pleased the ruler who had ordered his men to leave little if anything of value behind. The Doge, who ruled in the early 1500's, gifted this specific crown to his chief advisor for a job well done in their military campaigns.

Since The Doge had awarded it personally, the crown's value to his chief advisor's heirs was immeasurable not just monetarily but historically. The book's illustration depicted in detail a large crown fit for a king. I further read that it had been stored in a magnificent carved wooden box which had no illustration. This treasure, rumored to still be hidden in the residence of that chief advisor, at least as of this printing, had not been found. I wondered if it had been found since but decided I will have to check on that tomorrow at work.

With my magnifying glass, I examined every inch of the drawing again. The figures on the crown were indeed Byzantine. Two lean men dressed in the robes of the church sat like royalty on carved high back chairs. One reached for an angel, the other, prayed. The article stated the carved wooden box was lined in sterling silver and possessed a very unusual keyhole.

As I read further, I learned the chief advisor wore the crown to public events to demonstrate the Doge's approval of him. When that chief advisor became very ill, many wanted to steal the crown, but he had the forethought to hide it before he became too weak to walk and died. I turned the page surprised to see another handwritten note.

"Lana, this treasure still remains missing." *Still missing? Today?*

The crown disappeared in 1538 soon after the chief advisor's death. His family, hoping to inherit it, was unable to locate it. I flinched when my tea kettle whistled again breaking my train of thought. Why were all these books on Venice? It bothered me that a stranger might know about my Venetian lineage, ancestors, and perhaps even me. If that were so, those thoughts gave me the creeps.

Regardless, I was hooked and couldn't stop reading about the treasure. I took the book to bed with me and read until my eyes couldn't stay open any longer. I fell asleep wondering why whoever left the book believed this treasure would be of any significance to me. As I fell into a restless sleep, my dreams jolted between the crown, the odd shaped keyhole, and my handsome EMT. I imagined hearing his voice whisper in my ear. "I'm here with you, Lana. I'll always watch over you."

"Crash!" A loud noise from the street interrupted my wonderful dream. My mind fuzzy, my thoughts scattered, I woke from such a deep sleep like I had just awakened from anesthesia. Still, I tried to get a grip on my day. Oh no! With all these changes in my life, I forgot it was Wednesday, garbage collection day, and hadn't placed my own container on the street.

I glanced at the clock on my nightstand. Seven thirty. I overslept because I didn't hear my alarm clock ring. My blanket and extra pillow lay on the floor, the top sheet stretched all over the bed. My mind revisited my recent dreams concerned as to why they took such a hold on me. *Why does my handsome EMT continue to haunt me? Why do I think I hear him whisper in my ear? Why can't I get him out of my mind? Must stop thinking about him and reading those books if I hope to keep my job.*

I rushed to my small closet separated from my bedroom by a beaded curtain, threw on a brown dress, washed up, and raced out the door. I put my hairbrush and lipstick in my purse and grabbed a small bag of pretzels for lunch. I hated to be late. Fortunately, I lived only three blocks away. Even in my haste, I hoped to see my dream lover's vision and blinked hoping to see him all the way there. But no such luck.

Just like yesterday, patrons were already waiting in line to check out books. I plopped down at my desk, checked to make sure my roses had survived, and got to work. The first two in line were both elderly ladies and regulars. Retired, they were in no hurry and loved to chat. Suzanne, the taller of the two, looked very serious and spoke first. "Lana dear, we are desperate to read a good romance." She took a quick glance at the roses on my desk and pursed her lips. "Well, I can see by looks of things, especially those lovely roses, you must be in the middle of one yourself. Anyway, at our age, it's difficult to find a romantic lover so we thought we'd read and reminisce about our former trysts." Harriet, her friend, chuckled as she handed me their selections. "How did we do?"

Surprised by their choices, I responded. "If these were movies, they'd be R-rated. Are you both all right with that?" They giggled before Harriet answered. "You know we do need a little spice in our lives. Wait 'til you reach our age, you'll see."

Their chatter caused a slight but annoying delay for the others, but these women were so sweet and so much fun, I just put up with the whining of the library patrons who followed. Once I caught up with the line, I did a quick brush to my waist length hair and dabbed my lipstick. No time to finish because I spotted Tammy, the head librarian, heading toward my desk.

I winced. *I wonder if she noticed my peculiar behavior and that I was late two days in a row? And what about those beautiful enormous books. Maybe they were stolen, and I took them home thinking they were gifts for me. How would I have known otherwise? The notes were all addressed to me.*

Tammy stopped in front of my desk, lowered her glasses, and smiled. She didn't appear angry, on the contrary, her large blue eyes showed signs of genuine concern. Before I could explain anything about my behavior or those books, she asked in a sweet tone of voice. "Lana, I've noticed you've been acting a little odd these past few days. Is everything all right? If there's anything I can help you with, please tell me and I will make it my job to do so. After all, what's more important than the health and well-being of my staff?"

I looked up at her. Her deep blue eyes filled with kindness; her face reflected genuine reassurance. I took a deep breath, relieved it wasn't about the books. "I'm sorry. It seems I've gotten wrapped up in a history book so much so I stay awake reading longer than I should each night. I'll be more careful with my time in the future."

She placed her hand on my shoulder. "Please take care. I meant what I said. If there's anything at all you need, don't hesitate to ask. We're family here and must take care of one another." As she turned to return to her office, Tammy winked. "Nice roses by the way." She leaned over to smell the flowers and encouraged me. "You know I never want you to feel alone especially after all you've been through."

Tears flooded my eyes. "Thank you. That's very kind of you. I will reach out to you if I feel the need." I was surprised she noticed my unusual demeanor. I didn't want to say anything about my shadow visions, especially since I've had none so far today. Besides, she might think I've lost my mind and she's so wonderful to have as a supervisor. After she left, I looked at my cart. How could I forget about all those returns? So many....so early. *Don't these people have anything else to do first thing in the morning?*

I groaned a silent groan and left to put away all the returned books. I was in the "T's" when I noticed a young man who from behind looked like my handsome EMT. *Could it be him?* He turned when he heard me approaching with the cart. I looked at his face. No such luck...blue eyes...ruddy complexion...wrong nose. I must get that man out of my mind. Last night sure didn't help. I shelved all the books and returned to my desk. I chuckled to myself. *What no more new volumes?*

Either I must be getting greedy, or my secret admirer has given up. All those surprises were too good to be true.

Before I could sit down, a gentleman in the aisle next to the one I had just left cleared his throat as if trying to get my attention. I walked over to the end of that row and glanced down the aisle startled to see who was standing there. When he turned, his eyes met mine. I approached him stunned as he asked in a familiar tone of voice. "Excuse me, my lady, are you the librarian? I need to find a history book that covers The Venetian Republic between 1500 and1700."

I blinked. No shadow this time. My handsome EMT stood in front of me in the flesh. *Could this man really be him? I sure wanted him to be.* My jaw dropped so fast and hard it could have put a hole in the floor. From where I stood, this man bore such a striking resemblance to my EMT, he could be his twin. Same eyes, same sculptured haircut, my knees buckled before I could get my bearings to walk close to where he stood. I watched him search through the titles before I blurted out something stupid, unable to control my curiosity. "Have we met before? I think I know you. I'm sure I do. You work for the county EMT services, don't you?"

He avoided my question by opening a large book and reading its table of contents, but I was sure he was the one. Besides, he looked ever so handsome in a cranberry long sleeve shirt.

"Please, I have no idea what you're talking about. Help me find a book. I'm in a bit of a hurry." He spoke with that same delicious accent.

I nodded and motioned for him to follow me. "No problem. Please come with me sir." I led him to the section I knew would help his search. He pulled out a rather heavy book from a middle shelf and glanced through the table of contents before skipping through the chapters. "Thank you. This one might work."

"I'll be happy to check that out for you when you're ready." *After all, what woman wouldn't want to know his name?* "I'll just need you to answer a few easy questions."

He smiled. "I'm ready" and we walked back to my desk together. I tried not to stare but it was as hard as holding an ice cream cone and not taking a lick. I sat at my desk but before he handed me the book, I explained our library rules. "I'm happy I could be of assistance. For you to sign this out, all I'll need is one form of identification, a passport, driver's license, and anything with your name and photo on it...perhaps a school or work ID?"

This handsome man did an exaggerated search of his pockets and made a comical expression as he turned his trouser pockets inside out to show they were empty.

"Sorry. I lost my wallet and all my identification while travelling. Well, really, everything was stolen. My legal name is Marco Banelli, if that helps," He informed me with that sexy accent of his. Spanish? Perhaps Italian?

He continued to explain. "I lost it in Rome where some annoying young pickpockets robbed me on the grounds near the Coliseum. That place is loaded with them ready to take advantage of anyone they could get close enough to rob. I should have been more cautious. They touch you. You try to push them away, not wanting to hurt them because most are teenagers. When you take your hands out of your pockets, in go their hands as fast as lightning.

"You don't feel a thing and don't even realize you've been robbed until later when you need something from your wallet. They took my money and my wallet with all my credentials. I thought I was smart splitting up all those things and placing them in different pockets, but that didn't work. For fear of being robbed in an unfamiliar city, I carry no identification on me. Being a visitor to your city, I have no library card, so I guess I'll have to throw myself at your mercy, my lovely lady."

What did he just say? Could he have meant he left his credentials in his hotel room safe? His accent was delicious but at times hard to understand.

In all my years working at the library, his was by far the most creative excuse I had ever heard. Never having visited Rome, I wondered if his story held true. His wide eyes implied he was telling the truth. Of course, I was so smitten at that point I would have believed a dinosaur ate his wallet. I couldn't let this man I wanted to meet again escape from my life, so I decided to take a huge risk.

"Please Mr. Banelli, I need you to fill out a simple form and when you return the book, bring some form of identification back to me like a hotel receipt or any receipt with your name on it. Perhaps your airline ticket?"

I knew I was taking a big chance, but I wanted to get to know him better. "We're a local neighborhood library, and I have vouched for people many times before."

"Signora, please call me Marco. My English is not very good so it would be hard for me to fill out the form. Please sign this out to me. I give you my word of honor on the Banelli Family crest that I will bring it back to you before it's due."

He flashed another irresistible smile and stared deep into my eyes. I was so infatuated, how could I refuse? I know my decision was reckless, but I was dead sure his striking face was the same one I saw after my accident. If that's the case and he's too shy to tell me, I owe him for saving my life. So, I agreed before advising him.

"All right then. I will write your name on the form and personally vouch for you. Please give me the correct spelling and sign at the bottom. I'll allow you to take the book for one night only, but please don't let me down. Paying for a book like this would take a big bite out of my meager librarian's salary."

He did as I asked before looking at my name badge. He reached out to shake my hand. His hand felt smooth and warm and his handshake firm. "Thank you, Lana. I appreciate your kindness and understanding. Don't worry, I *will* see you tomorrow. In Venice, to a man of my position my word is my bond. Perhaps you'd allow me to take you out for a nice Italian dinner after you finish work tomorrow evening to express my appreciation and gratitude."

Odd, in an instant, his English became much better than he claimed. "That would be lovely, Marco." I answered in a calm fashion all the while my mind did mental summersaults. My dreams came true today. I met him in person and may see him again tomorrow.

After Marco left, I was so excited I wanted to call Aurellia as soon as I got home and tell her about Marco's visit. Even though he denied being an emergency worker, his resemblance to my mystery EMT was uncanny. Call it women's intuition, but I knew he was the one. Just thinking about him made my heart flutter and left me breathless. I'm certain he helped me at the accident scene. Since that was such an exhausting day, there's a slim chance I could be wrong, but I didn't think so. I guess I'll have to wait for him to return his book to confirm my suspicions. I hope with all my heart that I'm right because I want to see him again. And dinner? How much better can it get?

CHAPTER
THREE

After finally meeting Marco, I arrived home so excited it was hard to concentrate or catch my breath. I needed to calm myself and focus on this wonderful new event in my life. Tea always comforted me, so I went into my kitchen and put the tea kettle on. My mother always made me a special herbal tea. I had lost her in the accident, but I always kept a box of the tea in her memory. As I took it out along with the flowery pottery mug she gave me on my last birthday, the kettle's loud whistle jolted me back to reality. After a few sips, I thought about my mother's love and the new man in my life. I felt good enough to eat, so I made myself a tuna salad sandwich.

With no new volume to peruse tonight, I finished my dinner before working through selected chapters of the first two. I learned more about the rulers of Venice, their powers, and lavish lifestyle. I read that my ancestor knew The Doge of her time quite well along with the men who served in his inner circle and how different Doges sent armies to conquer distant places like Constantinople and Egypt. They ordered their troops to plunder valuable treasures and bring them back as spoils of war for the current Doge.

I love history so the facts kept me reading late into the night and fell asleep with my head on the open book. With all this new knowledge, I did not dream about the Doge or the Venetian Republic, instead romancing Marco filled my dreams.

The next morning came all too soon. A loud car horn woke me. I could have remained in my dreams with Marco all day. My head spun from too little sleep, and I had to cover my eyes from the bright sunlight which poured in around my window shades. Hoping to see Marco again, I wanted to look my best and decided to wear a fancier outfit than usual. I tried to remember how long it's been since I'd gone on a real date, but it's been too many years to count. I chose my special occasion dress, a royal blue and dark green flowered sundress with a ruffled hem and a blue jacket and positioned my locket where it would show best. I was extra careful with my make-up and spritzed myself with a light floral cologne. I wondered if Marco would really come back today and take me out to dinner like he promised.

Grabbing a quick lunch of peanut butter crackers, I walked to work all the while blinking for any sign of his shadow. Since there was none, I assumed he was the real deal. I arrived at my desk on time and not with my erratic tardiness. That alone should make my head librarian Tammy happy.

Returns, those dreadful returns from the night drop piled up on the side of my desk ready for me to catalog on my computer. When I finished, I filled my cart but couldn't reshelve all the books because patrons poured in earlier than usual. It was Thursday and they all said they were looking for an enjoyable read to escape all the dreadful news about the stock market on TV. I can't say I blame them.

After checking out their selections, I left my desk to put away the insurmountable number of returns. Finished, I approached my desk and watched our inter library loan delivery man place four large cardboard shipping cartons labeled

"Books-History Section" next to it. Ugh! Now, I would have to catalogue, barcode, and shelve all those new books. *I'm so glad I dressed for the occasion.*

Needing extra energy, I decided to have my lunch before I started. That has good points and bad because I always invite conversation whenever I sit at my desk for a break. I watched Mrs. Dufrene, a local, gray-haired widow who took a personal interest in me, look for a new read on historical fashion. She stopped when she spotted me having lunch and walked over. "My, my, Lana, you know in my youth I walked the fashion runways in New York and was a well sought after model. I wore Oscar de la Renta, Givenchy, and all the famous designers of that period. That's why I'm always interested in fashion both in the present and the past. I couldn't help but notice you're all dressed up today and look too nice to have plain old peanut butter crackers for lunch. Your beautiful roses still look so fresh, and you look as lovely as they do. Does your new outfit and those roses mean there's something exciting going on in your life? I do hope it's because you've met someone special."

I looked up from my lunch. "No Ma'am. I decided this morning that since I hadn't worn this dress for quite some time, I should wear it before it goes out of style."

"Well, my dear, that dress has classic lines, so no worries about that. It will stay in vogue for years to come. The green leaves accentuate the color of your eyes while the blue complements your ruddy complexion and red hair. Never mind how your locket sparkles against the dark hues. You're young, vibrant, and attractive. You should have a full social life. At any rate, stunning choice for no place to go and no one to share it with."

I shrugged my shoulders. "Thanks, I guess." She left soon after that to find her book. I ate the last bite of my crackers before I took a deep breath to prepare myself for the task at hand. I began to open each of the large cartons. When I finished, I counted twenty-nine books. I proceeded to enter each one on the computer, print out their labels with barcodes, and paste each label ready for checkout. I loaded them onto my cart and left my desk to shelve them. Odd, the entire time, I felt a pair of eyes follow my every movement. I turned and spotted that same thin man from the other day dressed entirely in black standing at the end of the aisle speaking to another patron. At least he wasn't a vision, someone else could see him. When he turned in my direction, his eyes laser fixed on me. It was as if he knew me. *Could he have seen my staff photo in the library's entrance?*

Tan, with a very distinctive thin, pointed nose, he appeared well-groomed, especially his thick black mustache. For whatever reason, he still gave me the creeps. I knew all our regulars but had never seen him before the other day. He smiled and saluted upon leaving. I returned to my desk happy to see him go. We live in a tourist area, so we do have some odd ducks visit every now and then. They usually prove to be creative types, writers, and artists.

After the stranger left, I looked up at the large black and white clock on the wall near my desk. Four forty-five? No Marco and he still had the library book I checked out to him. As I sat back beating myself up mentally for trusting him, I heard footsteps approach from the front entrance of the library. I gasped, hoping with my every breath it was him.

When I heard those footsteps turn my way, I crossed my fingers hoping it wasn't that odd man again. My heart skipped one more beat when I saw Marco. He was all smiles as he approached and handed me his book. "Lana, it was good but did not have all the information I needed. I need to find a different one to continue my research."

"Of course, but you have only a few minutes to find one

before the library closes." I responded, reminding him. "I hope we're still on for dinner."

He looked so continental and handsome, I was surprised I could speak in complete sentences. He winked. "We are. I have been looking forward to it all day. I will hurry to find another book before we must leave."

"You have five minutes."

"All right then, I will go back and select the first one I looked at yesterday. Will you still check it out to me?" He smiled his charming boyish smile.

How could I refuse? "Yes of course I will."

Marco made a mad dash for the same shelf he perused yesterday with books labeled The Venetian Republic 1500-1700. He returned soon carrying a thick volume entitled "The Doges of Venice 1530-1590" written in Italian. I checked it out to myself and gave it to him. Odd, I thought. He's researching the same location and time as those in my mystery volumes.

"Ah, I made it in time." He sighed. "The wall clock reads five o'clock on the dot. Do you have to close?"

I shook my head 'no.'

"Wonderful then, where I come from, it's too early for dinner. We could take a walk and stop for a glass of wine before we eat."

I blushed. "That would be wonderful. There's a park not too far from here and from there it's only a three-block walk to downtown where all the restaurants are."

Marco held out his arm for me. "Well, Lana, what are we waiting for, let's go." He placed his book under one arm and my arm in the other. I grabbed my purse happy not to have to close tonight or to carry any large volumes home with me. Marco was such a perfect gentleman he was too good to be true. He opened the front door of the library and escorted me down the stairs. I imagined I was a princess walking down a palace stairway because that was how special he made me feel. Still, I knew even a princess can't be too careful in the company of a stranger. As we walked to the park, I turned and blinked to make sure Marco wouldn't disappear, I so wanted him to be real. Marco noticed my paranoia. "Lana, are you expecting someone to follow us?"

"Only a Shadow Person." I laughed a nervous laugh.

"Shadow Person? What's that?" he asked as a puzzled expression crossed his face.

I winked and smiled. "Never mind, it's not as important as spending time with you."

Marco held my arm a little tighter. "Everything you do is important to me. A Shadow Person does not sound like much fun. Let's think about only happy thoughts tonight."

We walked to the park, found a bench, and watched the local world go by. All the semi-tropical flower gardens bloomed in colors of red, purple, and yellow. Dogs of all breeds and sizes chased each other around the park's small fountain. Young lovers stopped near the fountain to share a kiss oblivious to the rest of the world while high speed roller-skaters whizzed by our bench. Marco and I shared a laugh when we saw how one small dog took charge of walking his master before Marco changed the conversation to us. "Lana, it's so beautiful here and so warm. It's cold in Venice in February. I see why you love it here, but tell me, have you always lived in Florida?"

I squeezed his arm and felt bold enough to lean my head on his shoulder. "I have. I was born here in Naples, went to our local schools before leaving for the University of Florida in Gainesville. I returned after graduation to be close to my parents and sister."

My eyes swelled with tears. Marco handed me his handkerchief. He spoke in a soft tone. "By your expression, I take it they are no longer with you."

I wiped my tears. "They died in an auto accident. I suffered injuries as well. This locket is the only memory I have of them.

It belonged to my mother's ancestor." I paused. "I'm positive I saw an EMT after my accident that looked just like you."

Marco remained silent and avoided making eye contact with me. He looked down at his shoes not responding. When I finished that statement, he held my hands and looked into my eyes. "I don't think that could have been possible. I'm deeply sorry for your loss but our minds often see what they wish us to see.

"If you'd allow me, I'd like to tell you a little about my life. After I do, you'll understand how impossible it would have been for me to be here after your accident. I'm from Venice, Italy. That's why my intense interest in Venetian history. When my parents were alive, they served as long-standing patrons of the Venetian Historical Society. My ancestors held royal titles when they were allowed, and one even served as Chief Council to the ruling Doge of his time. That Chief Council was of royal lineage, a count, and as his direct descendant, if royal titles were still honored, I would hold that same title today."

He peeked over at me to see if he still had my attention. He did. I've been reading those large volumes too much because his story was beginning to sound just like one in those books.

Marco continued. "I live in that same Chief Council's palazzo that has passed down to a sole heir in each of my family's generations since his death. Marked by a historical plaque, the palazzo is an old building situated on the Grand Canal. Many of my ancestors, including my parents, have called that structure home. Venice is a most interesting and beautiful city not only because of our waterways but because of our unique history. Have you ever been there?"

I stared into his light brown penetrating eyes. "No, but I always wanted to go. My grandmother's ancestors were born in Venice. It can be a small world sometimes." I paused. "Paris has been on my wish list forever as well. I love to read travel magazines and any stories involving history. Tell me more about yourself, Marco. What do you do for work and what brought you here?"

He took my hand and kissed it. *Be still my fluttering heart.* "My lovely lady, we have much in common. You are Venetian by ancestry as am I and I do something similar to what you do for work. I am a researcher for a local treasure hunter who works in many of the grand old palazzos of Venice. Many of the long-standing former royal families such as mine believe previous generations stashed jewels, coins, old works of art somewhere in the hidden passageways, under roof beams, or in wall safes covered with plaster to make them appear as if they are part of the wall."

Hmm...that sounds familiar. I interrupted him. "I read about those treasures quite recently. Intriguing, you do know there have even been movies made about those types of adventures."

Marco puzzled again. "Moo-ovies? Cos'e quello? Sorry I mean what's that?"

I tried to explain. "You know moving pictures that tell a story."

He still looked like I made no sense at all. I was sure it was in my translation, so I said. "Never mind. Again, sorry for the interruption. Please tell me more."

He nodded. "First, I research the particular family's ancestry to see if anyone is royal like myself, went to war, and if any valuable artifacts, jewelry, or medals had been presented to them."

I listened but remained confused about one thing he said. "You just said if anyone is royal like yourself present tense, but just a few minutes ago, you said you were no longer considered royal." He laughed, "Sorry it's my English. I am of royal lineage but only by bloodline and personal history. The Italians no longer have ruling royals, but in my mind, I am still a count." Marco looked at his watch and changed the subject.

"It's six o'clock, time for that glass of Chianti I promised. Ready?"

I nodded. He smiled. "Wonderful. I know the perfect place." He placed his book under one arm, and we stood to walk two blocks off the beaten path from the park to a small Italian restaurant I never knew existed. Fuchsia bougainvillea and yellow hibiscus surrounded the stone walkway that led to the one floor, white, stucco building with a large brick patio covered by a red and white striped awning. Marco stopped at the edge of the patio to signal for a waiter to seat us.

"This is The Casa Rosetta, and I come here whenever my schedule allows. For me, it's like a taste of home. Chef Nunzio cooks like my grandmother."

A tall waiter dressed in a cranberry and white uniform greeted us with a distinct Italian accent. "Buongiorno Señor Marco or should I say Buono Sera. Welcome back. Please since we are not at all busy tonight, tell me where you and your beautiful guest would prefer to sit."

Marco knew at once. "Thank you, Antonio. We'd like to have a table on the outside patio under the large awning in case of evening showers."

The waiter walked us to our table and seated us. Marco then ordered our wine. "Two glasses of Chianti please and we'll start with the small antipasto platter before we order our dinners."

As soon as our waiter left, Marco turned to me. "I know we shouldn't ruin our appetites for dinner, but the antipasto here is too good to pass up. Besides, it gives us more time to talk and get acquainted."

Antonio returned shortly with our wine and appetizer platter. He poured the garnet red liquid into our glasses. Marco thanked him adding, "We'll need a few more minutes before we order. We'd like to enjoy our wine first."

The waiter nodded and left. We clicked glasses as Marco toasted. "To the loveliest lady I have ever met. May today be the beginning of a wonderful friendship." We only met yesterday but were so comfortable with one another it could have been a year. We chatted about anything and everything when Marco revealed, "I visited Florida a few months ago to get the lay of the land before selecting the right library for my research. This research is of foremost importance to me since at that time my elderly grandfather, who knew the most about our family history, asked me to investigate a specific treasure. He gave me clues based on verbal history passed down to him by my ancestors. I tried on many an occasion to keep a written record of these memories since he was the sole member of our family who possessed them, but he refused to allow it saying he didn't want to put me in any danger, what he was about to tell me was for my ears only.

"Grandfather then proceeded to tell me that in the early 1500's my family's present palazzo served as another Chief Council's' residence. As was the custom, each Doge in Venetian history desired his Republic to become a major military conqueror and would send his army to fight in distant places. Any valuable treasures plundered were to be returned to the Doge of that time.

"One such treasure, an ancient gold and platinum crown dating back to the early 1200's, was one of the many spoils of war brought back for a previous Doge. Venetians have always been lovers of art and history, so all the treasures returned to Venice intact. That Doge stored the crown for safety in a wooden box made of fruitwood. Many years later, one of his successors had the box hand painted by a famous artist of the early sixteenth century to present this treasure to his Chief Advisor as a special engagement gift along with the key to unlock it, a reward for his loyal and dedicated service to the Republic."

Marco glanced over to see if I was still interested. I was and became mesmerized by his every word since his story could have been torn right out of the volume I was reading. Marco sensed that and continued. "His Chief Advisor Sergio Casselli, of royal lineage, and an ancestor on my grandmother's side, was young, twenty-two at that time, ambitious, and head over heels in love. In 1517, he asked a beautiful young lady of similar social standing to marry him. When she agreed, he gave her a hand-crafted piece of jewelry, a pendant loaded with gemstones to celebrate their upcoming wedding and advised her to keep it safe as their destiny depended on it. Her pendant possessed a special hidden key. That special key was the only way anyone could open that beautiful wooden box without breaking into it.

"Sergio, whose first name aptly means attendant, never expected the couple's parents to feud and cause their break-up. Since the Doge advised his betrothed to keep the pendant, Sergio was no longer able to unlock the box and obtain the valuables inside. Years passed and that Chief Advisor still hoped to find his lover and her pendant, but when he became extremely ill at age forty-five, he hid the box in our family palazzo to prevent his enemies from stealing it. My grandfather further told me that I had the right to claim both treasures because he willed the residence to me.

"With his blessing, I combed every inch of my family's palazzo. I tried to imagine where I would hide such a treasure to keep it safe from my enemies. After much thought, I was fortunate enough to find what I believed to be the box in question."

I listened, remembering what I read in those two large volumes. The roses...the odd figure dressed in black? *Coincidence? Conspiracy?* Oddly, Marco's story sounded exactly like one of the stories I had just read. As those thoughts swirled in my mind, he continued.

"I came here to Naples guided solely by the fact that my now late grandfather believed a distant relative of Sergio's fiancé resided here and may have the key to that box. It's a long shot and a long way to come for such a small item so I can guess your next question. Why don't you just pry the box open? Well, the answer is not so easy. Have you heard of the Italian artist named Raphael?"

I nodded. "Of course, I have. Are you trying to tell me that he was the artist who hand painted the outside of the box? If that's so, I don't think I would pry it open either. That box is also a treasure."

"It is indeed. Few people realize Raphael painted a few of his larger works on fruitwood supports. Grandfather told me The Doge commissioned Raphael to paint that fruitwood box as an engagement present for my ancestor and locked the crown inside to secure the young couple's future. This small chest had delicate leaves painted in 18K gold on both its sides. On the top, Raphael painted a wedding couple in the full ceremonial dress of the time surrounded by a wreath of flowers. My grandfather never saw the treasure, his own grandfather only passed down a description but never its location. Grandfather said he swore to keep this information a secret to protect the family treasure from Venetian thieves. That is why he did not want a record of this information left for anyone to read. He advised me about it because of his failing health, and I was his only heir.

"So, as you can see, to pry the box open would destroy not only a family treasure, but one that also belongs to the art history world as well. That's why I must find the proper key to open it."

I sat back and took a deep breath. Marco's story sounded like one of the romance novels I loved to read but my mind wandered off deep in thought about the uncanny correlation to the history book left on my desk. Those thoughts disturbed me until I heard a sudden "Crash." A loud, reverberating metal noise from the kitchen shook us both back to reality. Marco jumped up from his seat while I gasped before turning to see a tall, thin man, his face covered by shadows standing further back under the awning staring at us. *Why is that man staring at us?*

Antonio noticed Marco's unusual behavior and ran over to explain. "I apologize for the abrupt interruption. Our newest dishwasher dropped a large tray of silverware. Sorry again for that annoyance. Please allow me to refill your glasses on the house."

Marco took a deep breath and calmed down. "Thank you. Not a problem. I fence and the noise sounded just like the clanging of swords. For a moment, I forgot where I was."

Did I hear that right? He fenced? The waiter returned at once with the Chianti bottle and refilled our glasses. Marco waited for him to leave before he continued his story.

"I did locate a beautiful, hand-painted box that matched my grandfather's description hidden in an unusual location but can't be sure if it contains the crown until I open it. Before I arrived here, I searched every inch of my palazzo for that key, the pendant, but it was not there or anywhere in the other historic palaces in Venice I had to investigate for my work. For fear of damage or theft to both treasures, I placed the box back in its original hiding place before I came here."

By this point, I felt like I was smackdab in the middle of an Indiana Jones movie or at least in the pages of the large history volume that consumes my nights. Dusk crept over the patio as our waiter returned to light the candles on our outside table. The red and green lanterns around the patio roof came on like magic. I looked into Marco's golden-brown eyes. They were dreamy or at least to a wall flower librarian who doesn't get out very often, well not at all, to meet sexy men. Marco's voice was deep yet soft, and I became hypnotized by his melodic tones until our waiter awakened me from my reverie. "May I take your order, Ma'am?"

Marco looked at me. "Please Lana, I eat here often. Allow me to order for you." He removed the menu from my hands. I was so taken by his chivalry, I didn't have the strength to say "no," so I nodded as he instructed Antonio.

"To start, we'll have two cups of Italian wedding soup followed by two small plates of angel hair pasta in the orange cream sauce with shrimp. I'd like to order veal Masala as our main course with a salad to follow and please bring us another bottle of Chianti to share with our meal. We are not in any hurry so we would appreciate extra time between courses. Thank you." The waiter nodded before he took the menus and returned shortly with the wine and our soup.

The aromas of the different dishes, the dim lighting under the bright moonlight, not to mention my dreamy date, intoxicated my senses. I became spellbound as he discussed the customs of Venice at the time of the missing treasure and of course more about himself. He put me at ease, so I revealed more about myself to him. As I spoke, Marco's eyes left mine to concentrate on my necklace. "What a lovely pendant. That's quite an unusual shape. May I take a closer look?"

I nodded. He held the chain up to the candlelight to examine the pendant more closely. "It's beautiful. Antique Italian pendants shaped in odd and ornate ways often served a double duty. By the gold filigree work, it does appear old and may have been created in Venice. You said your grandmother's ancestor was from Venice?"

He held onto the chain as I answered. "I really know little about her or my pendant. Since it's all I have left of my ancestry, I take the best care of it. The one thing I do know is that it has been in my family for many generations, and the eldest daughter in each generation inherited it along with the right to wear it. I always wondered what if anything was inside but was afraid to open it lest I or a jeweler break the pendant or its chain. I am half Italian and half Scottish hence the red hair and green eyes."

Marco smiled and let the necklace drop back down on my

dress. "Your curly red hair could be a Northern Italian trait as well. Your pendant is as exquisite as you are."

We ate, drank wine, and talked until the restaurant staff prepared to close. Marco took my hand. "Come, they're telling us it's closing time. We should leave after all we don't want to overstay our welcome. If you like, we can come back tomorrow night."

If I like? What woman in her right mind wouldn't like. I nodded and proceeded to get up. Marco signed for the check, and we walked home under the light of a full moon. When we reached my apartment house, we stopped by the front entrance. I looked into his sexy eyes. "Marco, thank you for the most wonderful evening. I look forward to tomorrow night as well."

Marco whispered in my ear. "Until then, my sweet lady, my heart will count the seconds." He gently placed his hand under my chin and drew my face close to his. His eyes filled with passion as he leaned in for a quick kiss. My heart raced, my head swirled. He sensed I wanted more because the next time his lips met mine, he gave me a longer more passionate kiss. My knees weakened when he deepened the kiss.

We held that kiss for a while before he pulled me closer for an embrace that molded our bodies into one. I opened my eyes to find his eyes gazing back into mine. As our lips parted, I thought I saw steam fill the air between us.

We caressed and kissed once more before I stepped back, concerned my heart would overtake my head. Not a smart thing for a woman to do since he still was a stranger, and this was our first date. I gave his hand a gentle squeeze.

"Marco, thank you again. I've had such a wonderful time and enjoyed a most memorable evening. I will see you tomorrow, but I must go. I do have to get up early for work."

I kissed the tip of his nose before walking up the few steps to the front door of my apartment building. After I unlocked the door, I turned to watch him walk away, but I must not have been quick enough because I didn't see him at all. It was like he disappeared into the night air. Still drunk with infatuation, I chalked up missing him go to my slow reflexes.

I went inside to my small apartment, my head filled with the most romantic evening of my life, the most handsome man I have ever met, and just as in my book, the intrigue of hidden royal treasures in a Venetian palace. Combined with half a bottle of Chianti at dinner, I had no trouble falling asleep that night in my own bed and not on the kitchen table.

CHAPTER
FOUR

Happy to be with the alive Marco and not his shadow, I walked to the library the next morning with vigor. I couldn't wait to get there and once at my desk, time flew as I chatted with patrons who were surprised by my new attitude. My old self was tired of listening to stories about their interesting lives, but since my life has now become interesting, my perspective on everything has changed.

Mr. Downing, a regular library patron who has travelled the world many times over, stopped by my desk. "Lana, please help me find a book on the history of Easter Island. I was fortunate enough to visit the island three years ago and saw firsthand those enormous statues called Moais. Easter Island is one of the most remote islands in the world and a World Heritage Site."

He took out his cell phone and showed me some photos from his trip including one of him standing beside one. "Wow, that's amazing. What exactly are you trying to research?" I asked.

"Since I've been reviewing these photos from the trip, I realized I'd like to know more about the Rapa Nui people and how and why they created these large figures. Someone told me they were markers for the graves of their kings. I'd like to verify that fact and read more about their royals. Funny, how when I visited and toured the island for four days, I never thought about those things. The Moai statues were so massive, so tall, they took your breath away just admiring them."

"In order to help you. I'll have to do some research. That's not an everyday request and one with which I'm not familiar. I'll have to search my library guide for the location of books on that subject. Please come back to my desk with me and wait while I search." My research took about fifteen minutes but as soon as I found some books that would help, I walked him to the appropriate section and left him with several of them to peruse.

Returning to my desk, I was so smitten with the fact that Marco was a real person, I didn't pay any attention to where I walked. I bumped straight into another patron farther down that same aisle. Even though I was on a mission to get back to work, I wanted to be polite, so I said. "Excuse me, sir."

When I turned to get a better look, that odd stranger from the other day stood next to me and stared into my eyes. Today he wore a red silk, long-sleeved shirt medieval in style and had the audacity to wink at me. *I wondered if that was his trademark move with women. I wasn't interested. He had a long way to go to catch up to Marco.*

"No problem, my exquisite lady. I'm always delighted to see you," he responded. As before, he bowed, waving his arm forward and stepping aside to allow me to pass. The stranger exhibited peculiar behavior but after working with the public for so long, I've seen just about everything. After he left, I dubbed him "Sir Mystery Man" to myself. Funny, now that I've met the real-life Marco, I wasn't concerned about his shadow today, even my "Sir Mystery Man" didn't daunt me. Amazing what falling in love can do for a lonely librarian. I haven't felt this happy since college when Mike Brimley and I fell in love sophomore year. We thought we could walk on clouds until a cheerleader named Bunny crossed our paths. So much for Mike's love. So much for Bunny. I walked back to Mr. Downing to see if he needed any more help, but he found the book he wanted. We took it to my desk together to check it out. I looked up at the clock. Four fifteen... Thank goodness. Not too much longer until I see Marco.

We chatted all the way back to my desk about his research when I stopped short and gasped. My face blushed as I called out. "What's this? Who would do such a thing?"

That sudden drastic change to my demeanor only became worse when I saw everything from the top of my desk in a pile on the floor, while another large volume opened to a specific page positioned at its center with my last few remaining roses shifted further to the right. Mr. Downing tried to reassure me because I'm sure he could see how upset I was. He touched my arm. "Looks like some mean-spirited library patron made more work for you. Good thing you're young and energetic and not my age."

Shaken, I checked out Mr. Downing's book as quickly as I could. Besides being off guard, I was curious and wanted to examine the newest edition "Volume Three: The Treasures of the Doges." I looked at the title of the open chapter "The Mysteries of the Missing Treasures" and perused its pages quickly, but the more I read, the more I realized the story was identical to the one Marco had recounted last night. Of course, without any of his personal details, and the article also included all the missing treasures of other Doges.

I read how hidden inside the Chief Council's palazzo was a valuable crown from ancient Istanbul, then Constantinople, made of 18K gold and platinum. No one has seen hide or hair of this crown since the death of that Chief Council named Sergio Castelli, again a name and facts Marco had mentioned last night. As of this printing, many scholars of antiquities believe this treasure, stored in an exquisite box, remains buried somewhere in that residence. The two families, that of the late Sergio Castelli and that of the Doge, himself, both laid claim to the crown and treasured box after Castelli's death. I found it amusing that the family of the Doge who gifted the crown to his late advisor wanted to go against The Doge's own wishes and take it back. I guess when money was involved, nothing was off the table. The family of the late Sergio Castelli was so affluent they decided to buy the property from the Republic paying way over its true value hoping to lay claim to that treasure for their subsequent heirs.

Count Marcello, the ink blurred over his last name, was the second resident of royal lineage to live in this palazzo and to serve as Chief Advisor to a Doge. No such treasure was recorded as found while he resided there.

The crown's value converted to present day market price was worth more than ten million dollars not only for its gold and platinum value but for the intricate carvings across the front of the crown depicting two ancient priests in ornate long robes. *That estimate did not include Raphael's priceless hand painted box not even mentioned in this article. The provenance of that treasure alone was immeasurable.* This volume had an artist's rendering of what the crown looked like, but nothing at all about that small wooden chest.

Marco had told me everything he knew about that small chest. I read as much as I could at work, but the text contained no description of Raphael's work. I remembered Marco said he'd found a small chest matching his grandfather's description but couldn't open it. *There were too many coincidences regarding this story to ignore. Why was this third book placed on my desk? Come to think of it, why were any of them?*

The timing of this book's appearance was intriguing, especially so soon after Marco's story. Could someone other than Marco be interested in this crown? Could that be the same person who had sent me the books?

I must ask Marco about these coincidences when I see him later. Placing a piece of white typing paper to mark the page, I closed the large volume and tried to go about business as usual, but that became more difficult considering all these new events.

Like clockwork, Marco appeared at four forty-five with his library book in hand. As our eyes met, the sparks of last night's passion continued to fly between us. I hoped no one nearby noticed our loving looks. He winked, flashing his irresistible smile. I tried not to notice his charm since I needed answers, but that was impossible. He brought his return to my desk along with a book of illustrations of crowns from that period to check out as well.

I touched his hand hoping to keep him close. "Marco, you must see this." I whispered. "Please stand behind me and look at what someone left on my desk." I opened the book to that marked page and pointed to an artist's rendering of what the crown looked like. "Does this look like the crown you hope to find?"

As Marco walked behind me and touched my shoulder, I thought my heart would burst right out of my chest. He studied the drawing for a few minutes before he commented.

"This is just a sketch. Since no one had found the crown and there was only word of mouth descriptions, the artist had to guess. Remember I said one sees what the mind wants us to see. It looks similar but is not an exact match to my grandfather's description. Does it say that Count Marcello Banelli, was the last one to see this?"

I shook my head. "No. I read no one has seen it since Castelli's death, but the ink was blurred when it mentioned a Count Marcello."

"Interesting. Count Marcello and I have a history together. I will explain later. There's too much to tell here..."

I blushed, a bit embarrassed, wondering what he thought of

my curiosity about him. He glanced at the page again. "Is this book a library book?"

I whispered so no one would overhear. "No. This book as well as two other editions were gifts from an anonymous patron to me."

Marco beamed. "I'm jealous. Someone else must have noticed your beauty. That's a very generous gift. The book is an antique, a first edition, and has a gold leaf border. I'd be interested in reading some of the chapters but for tonight, let's leave your book here. We can take it home and examine it more closely tomorrow." He smiled and lifted his shoulders. "Who knows? We might find clues or a note in there about who gave you those beautiful volumes. Tonight, I promise I will tell you everything I know about Count Banelli, but he's not at the top of my list because our dinner is. I have a special surprise for you."

"A surprise?" I beamed anxious to learn what it was.

"Yes." He answered. "You'll find out soon. I'll wait for you outside after you close the library,"

I closed the book and left it on my desk before I closed the library as fast as lightning. Rushing outside to meet him, my mind worked overtime wondering what his surprise could be. I met him at the bottom of the steps, and he walked me around the side of the building before he said.

"Our plans for tonight are special. A romantic picnic under the stars and near the water. I'll go and load our basket with wine and goodies before I pick you up at your apartment in one hour so we can walk to the canal in the park close to your house. I am looking forward to spending time with you alone under the moonlight."

"That sounds wonderfully romantic," I sighed.

I rushed home and slipped into something more feminine before Marco arrived on time exactly one hour later carrying a large wicker picnic basket. He kissed me and said, "Let's go find our stars."

I grabbed his arm, and we walked the short four blocks to the park. He stopped at a secluded area I had never seen before with no picnic table and placed the basket down on the grass before he gave me another quick kiss. Taking a light blanket from the basket, he spread it over the grass before he reached for my hand and kissed it. "Lana, you make me the happiest man in the world." He held onto my hand. "Please let me help you sit."

I knew I didn't need help, but his offer was so chivalrous, I held his hand. He sat down next to me and removed a small bag of three grapes from the basket. He took one out at a time and fed them to me, kissing my lips after each one. The kisses got longer and more passionate with each grape. I looked into his light brown eyes. He knew I wanted more but reminded me. "Remember, we are saving our love for dessert."

I laughed. "You know I have a short memory," I said, before I kissed him again with a passion as deep as our feelings. As he wrapped his muscular arms around me, my heart melted from the heat of our passion. When our lips released, I teased. "Marco did you inherit those strong arms from Count Banelli?"

He laughed and waved his finger up and down. "I already told you those amazing stories will come later but for now we have a wonderful picnic to enjoy."

Marco then removed two wine glasses and a bottle of red which he had already uncorked. He filled our glasses before he proposed a toast. "Lana, you have stolen the key to my heart just like someone stole the key to that treasure. I want you to keep me in your heart always as I will keep you in mine."

I reached over and stroked his black hair. "I can't wait to enjoy our picnic, everything you do for me is wonderful."

Marco grinned as he took out matching plates and silverware before adding the sliced cheeses, Italian bread and ham, grapes, and strawberries. He arranged two dishes, and we enjoyed our dinner under a setting sun in private away from the walkers, skateboarders, and dog walkers. As dusk settled in and after we finished our meal, Marco took my hand and kissed it. He moved closer to me on the blanket, caressed, and kissed me. As his kisses softly moved down my neck, my body burned with desire for him. He held onto my waist, and we lay down on the blanket together caressing, lost in the throes of our passion. He looked into my eyes and whispered, "Lana, I'm so happy we found each other. You complete me and make me whole."

We kissed once more before Marco advised. "It's getting dark. I think it may be time to leave. I'll walk you home and keep you safe. Tomorrow evening, I have even bigger plans for us."

Bigger plans? How wonderful! I can't wait!

We walked back under a starlit sky holding hands and not saying a word until we reached my front door. He gently took my face in his hands and softly kissed each cheek, then moved those kisses to the tip of my nose, until he reached my lips with the most loving kiss I have ever experienced in my life. "Rest well my love. I will see you tomorrow in the library. I have another special evening planned for us." He blew me a kiss before he walked down the street. Infatuated with his love, I could barely open the front door to the apartment house. Once inside, I threw myself on the couch burning with the memory of a sweet love-filled evening and thinking how I could hardly wait until tomorrow.

CHAPTER
FIVE

The next day, I found it difficult to concentrate. All I could think about was our romantic tryst last night. I plodded through the returns, chitchatted with regular customers, all the while wondering how Marco would surprise me tonight. I couldn't wait to see him. As the afternoon progressed, I kept one eye on the clock until it finally read four forty-five. On time, he entered through the main entrance, turning the head of every woman he passed.

Marco winked and brought his return to my desk. He leaned over and whispered in my ear, "My plans do not allow enough time for reading tonight. They only include our love."

I smiled, not knowing how to answer, especially in front of any nosey patrons. Marco continued, "I have already cooked a wonderful Italian dinner for the two of us in my favorite restaurant's kitchen and left it in their oven to stay warm. As soon as I leave you, I'll pick everything up and meet you at your apartment as soon as I can."

I clapped my hands. "That's a wonderful surprise! I can't wait to have it. Were you in the restaurant's kitchen all this afternoon?'

"I don't have too much extra time to explain my cooking

methods because I must go get our dinner so we can enjoy it while it's hot."

Regardless of his lack of response, I still was elated. I never had a man cook dinner for me or breakfast or lunch for that matter and it all sounded so romantic. Once we were outside the library, I kissed Marco on the cheek and headed straight home hoping I'd have enough time to clean up my messy apartment before he arrived.

What a mess! That thought didn't do it justice. It was much worse than I remember. I quickly cleared my kitchen table picking up odds and ends and putting everything away. Lucky for me, I had just enough time because as soon as I rinsed the last coffee mug and placed it in the dishwasher, the buzzer to the outside door sounded. Since I lived on the first floor, I dashed out into the front hallway and opened the door to let Marco in.

He announced as soon as he entered. "My lady, our dinner has arrived."

I greeted him with a big smile and held my apartment door open so he could bring in a large cardboard box. Whatever was inside smelled scrumptious! Marco placed the carton with care on my kitchen counter. He removed a bottle of wine, and something wrapped in foil. I drooled as he told me about our dinner. "Lana, I prepared one of my family's favorites. Deep dish lasagna with extra marinara sauce, crusty Italian bread I kept warm by placing it over the foil wrapped lasagna dish, some delicious cannoli for dessert, and of course a bottle of Chianti. As soon as we set the table, I hope you'll enjoy my culinary efforts."

At once, I went to my kitchen cabinet and removed two mismatched red and white plates, two wine glasses, napkins, and silverware and set the table. Before Marco put the empty carton on the floor, he further surprised me by pulling from the box a wide red candle, some matches, and a wine opener from his pocket. After placing the candle in the center of the table, he lit it and uncorked the wine. What a romantic start to the evening! Both the food and wine smelled and looked as delicious as he did.

We ate, drank wine, and had the tastiest chocolate chip cannoli for dessert before Marco began to chat about what Count Banelli was like.

Marco began the count's story by saying. "You know, the count and I share the closest of bloodlines." He chuckled but I had no idea what was so funny. Marco then teased me with tidbits about the count's life. "Grandfather told me Count Banelli, proud of his family history, wanted to be addressed by his royal title, and loved his hunting dogs more than some of his relatives because, as he always said, they would never double cross him. He loved very expensive jewelry that had to be hand-crafted in Venice by our local master jewelers of his time."

Being a history buff, I enjoyed listening to all the trivia about the count, but this small amount of information was not enough to quench my interest. After Marco finished telling me those anecdotes about the royal, he helped me put the remaining food in the fridge while I loaded the dishwasher. Marco held me by my waist, turned me around, and shot me one of his irresistible smiles.

"It's time for us to go sit on the couch and get comfortable. We can finish this bottle of wine while I reveal more to you about Count Banelli."

We carried our glasses to my coffee table before we sat down on the sofa. Marco brought the wine bottle and refilled them. He toasted. "To a wonderful evening with the most interesting and lovely lady I have ever met."

He leaned over for a quick kiss. I was more than happy to oblige. He put his glass down on my coffee table and took mine out of my hands and placed it there as well. I felt his arms reach around my waist as he pulled me closer to him. I could tell by the look in his eyes exactly what he had in mind. "It's time for us to get to know each other better. We can finish this bottle of wine and afterwards I'll reveal more to you about Count Banelli."

His touch was gentle as he caressed my body. I wanted to push him away but didn't have the willpower. "Marco, please, I can't, we haven't known each other long enough. Besides I thought we were going to talk about Count Banelli." I managed to get that out before Marco whispered, "Oh, that old fellow, he can wait."

He slowly nibbled my neck before moving his lips up to meet mine again. We kissed with such passion, our lips refused to let go. He deepened the kiss and with the softest touch pushed me to lie down on the couch. Marco embraced me, kissing my ear while he unbuttoned my blouse. Again, I tried to stop him, but his touch was so tender. I was smitten and felt like I was in a coma from my passion. My mind knew I should never do this on a third date, but my body begged otherwise. I burned with longing for him. Marco's lips felt warm and smooth as they moved down from my ear to my neck, then down to my breasts. He gently kissed and caressed them until they ached with desire.

Paralyzed by my longing for him, I couldn't move. He stared deep into my eyes. "Please Lana, let me show you how much you mean to me." I nodded before he stood, held out his hands, and helped me stand. I was so taken by his loving ways, I allowed him to undress me until I stood naked and exposed to a man I had only known for three days yet yearned for with my every breath. I wanted him to stare at my body and did not try to cover myself. At this point, I didn't care about "proper rules." I desired him and had fallen in love with him no matter how brief our relationship. I lay down and he did the same facing me. He softly whispered in my ear. "Lana, I'm falling in love with you. My body desires yours. Please let me show how much I love you."

I whimpered a weak "yes" before he began to please me. His hands were so gentle, his lips, as soft as silk as he kissed and caressed every inch of me. My body warmed from his every move like being in the sun. When his lips touched mine again, he deepened the kiss. I looked into his eyes as he stared down at my naked body with desire and longing.

I, too, was burning with that same deep yearning. I had never experienced anything like this before. Marco stood and undressed. His body muscular and tanned, he lay down on top of me and caressed me before we made love. We both became lost in the throes of our passion. Every part of me throbbed. We made love once more before we both fell asleep.

I awoke in the middle of the night amazed to find my dream lover gone. I glanced over at the coffee table, surprised to see a long-stemmed red rose with a note underneath. I picked up the note to see it written in long hand with fresh black ink, like from a fountain pen.

My Dearest Lana,

I'm in love with you. You have just given me the most romantic night of my life. I hope you feel the same. You are in my thoughts every second and I cannot get you out of my mind. I hope we can meet tomorrow after you close the library. When we do, I will tell you more about me. Besides, I have another surprise for you. We will meet at the library and walk to that same park bench.

You fill my heart with love and passion. I hope to show you how much again tomorrow.

With love always,
Marco

PS I'm leaving this very small hourglass with its shifting sands to show you how brief our time together may be. Remember no one knows for sure how long their time on earth will be.

Where did he get the rose? It was beautiful. And the hourglass? When did he leave? We slept so close together, I'm sure I would have felt him get up. My lover was full of surprises. *What more does he need to tell me?* With those thoughts as well as memories of our romantic evening swirling in my mind, I put my head back down on the couch pillow wondering what tomorrow would reveal.

CHAPTER
SIX

That next morning, I awoke from a very sensual dream, one in which Marco and I were in Venice. It was nighttime and we hid under some blankets in a gondola moored in a quiet side canal making love. As those sweet thoughts of Marco filled my mind, my body trembled every time I smelled the faint scent of his cologne which still lingered on my sofa pillows. I wanted to stay there all day but knew I had to get up early even though it was a Saturday. I had promised to cover for another librarian who was maid of honor at her sister's wedding. She was always so nice to me, so of course, I was happy to help. I showered, picked out a green and gold knit dress, packed my lunch, and hurried to the library.

Once settled at my desk, I took a deep breath and composed myself ready for my workday. Like lightning, a German shepherd named Zeus, a leader dog belonging to a blind patron Gary Black, placed his two front paws on my desktop and put the soft handles of my lunch tote in his mouth ready to drag it onto the floor. He must have smelled my roast beef sandwich and decided he'd like to try it for a snack. I stood just as Gary said "Stop Zeus. I'm sorry, Lana. I heard him jump and figured he was up to no good. He's usually better behaved."

I laughed, "No worries. He's such a great dog, if I wasn't so hungry I'd be happy to give him my lunch." Zeus looked at me, wagged his tail, and smiled his adorable smile. He knew I kept a small box of dog biscuits in my desk drawer. He even knew the right drawer because he came over to it and pawed it. I opened the box and gave him one along with a big hug. He was so sweet, I couldn't help myself, especially because I've known him ever since he was a puppy.

I took my lunch tote along with me for security and went into our break room to get a cup of coffee. As I walked back to my section, I heard a loud thud. *Zeus again?* I ran back to see what happened. *Could that be?* Another large book sat on the floor to the right of my desk chair. Volume Four: "The Royals and Rulers of Venice" was face up on the floor with a page marked by a gold leaf bookmark and left open for me to see. How on earth will I be able to lift that book onto my desktop? Never mind how I'll get these last two volumes home. I looked to see if anyone was around to help me, but no one was nearby. Within mere seconds, that unusual mustached man appeared at the end of the row visible from my desk. He smiled, winked, and approached me. I froze because of his odd manner. Dressed all in black, he continued to walk straight towards me.

"You look especially lovely today, my lady. I don't want you to struggle with that heavy book. Would you like me to help lift it onto your desktop?"

I smiled and nodded. At that point I was so desperate, I would have accepted help from Frankenstein.

"Please allow me." He leaned down and lifted the heavy volume with ease placing it with the other at center of my desk. *Where do all these muscular men come from?*

"I positioned them in numerical order. Volume Four is on top." He proceeded to open the book to the designated page.

"Thank you for your help. I never could have done that by myself." I told him. He responded. "You're most welcome.

Every time I see you, I can't help but notice your beauty and that beautiful pendant around your neck. It's as lovely as you are. That pendant looks like a treasured antique. Am I right?"

I did not respond. Proud of my ancestry, I always wore it on the outside of my outfit. Besides, that was none of his business, but that didn't stop him from continuing.

"If you ever think of selling the locket, I would like to buy it and am willing to pay a grand price. One that would surpass any amount issued from a jewelry appraisal." He reached over to touch my necklace. I pulled back holding my pendant in my hand, but this stubborn man would not leave. He stepped close enough to brush against my desk and glanced down at the open page. "Ah Venice, that city is the most intriguing city in the world to me. Have you been there? I've heard many secrets still rest in those old buildings on the Grand Canal."

I covered the open page with the morning newspaper a patron left me and responded with a defiant "no," but he still refused to stop. "Remember my offer is good any time. Think long and hard about it. Oh, and I believe you *will* visit Venice sooner than you think. I must warn you when you do, you'll find out that handsome man of yours is not who he says he is."

My stomach became uneasy with his last remark. My hands trembled as I thought about calling another librarian in for help. I became curt hoping my bad attitude would encourage him to leave. "I'm sorry, sir. If there is not a book you need help finding or checking out, I have work to do. I appreciate your help, but I must ask you to leave my desk."

"A book?" he pondered before pointing to Volume Four. "How about that one?"

His remark further annoyed me. I flushed with anger. "You may not have that one. It is a gift for me. It does not belong to the library. Please leave or shall I call security?"

He grinned. "I know that's a gift and can guess who sent it.

Someone is watching over you, so I must issue another warning. Be careful what you wish for. Things are not as they seem."

With that he turned and left. We don't have any security guards, but I had to threaten him with something. Thank goodness it worked. Anyway, what kind of nonsense was that? He gave me the creeps, so I was relieved when he left. Could he be my secret admirer? I sure hope not. I took a deep breath to calm myself down from this strange encounter. Lucky for me, Mrs. Townsend stopped by as soon as that crazy man left.

"Hi Lana, strange bird that one. I've seen him in the library the last few days. If you're thinking of dating him, please be careful. This morning, I found him sitting on the library steps singing Italian love songs while strumming a mandolin or so he claimed. I don't understand Italian."

I laughed. "Don't worry. He's not my type, but I appreciate your concern."

Mrs. Townsend breathed a loud sigh of relief. "Thank goodness. I became worried because I noticed you're all dressed up again. I figured a date might have something to do with your choice of wardrobe. Anyway, I'm always glad to help. We single women must stick together. It's been so difficult since I lost my Stanley."

She pulled a tissue from her purse and wiped her eyes. I stood to give her a hug. "I remember how devastated you were. Losing someone you love changes your entire outlook on life. I know firsthand from losing my parents and sister in an accident."

Mrs. Townsend wiped her tears with a lace handkerchief. "And I remember the kindness you showed me during that time, bringing me books to read and that lovely bouquet of flowers was so thoughtful and beautiful. When I started to accept what happened, my daughter-in-law's friend Katia suggested I try to meet someone nice just as a friend over coffee. She suggested an online site called 'Meet Your Golden Match' and helped me post my information since I'm not internet savvy. I still can't believe I allowed her to do that. but she was so sweet and wanted me to be happy. You know how conservative I am and at that time considered myself still in mourning, but Katia said this would be good for me, so I went along with it."

"How did you like that site? Did you meet anyone nice?"

"Well, it's a bit of a long story. Katia followed their rules and posted an up-to-date photo of me, as well as honest data about my age, background, likes, dislikes, etc. The service goes through your data and sends you six matches in your area that might suit you before they arrange a meeting over coffee."

"You now have me hooked. Did you find a suitable coffee date?"

Mrs. Townsend chuckled. "You're not going to believe what happened next. I looked at the first photo and was shocked to find that it was my next-door neighbor Evie's present husband. They are not divorced so why on earth would he be looking for someone else?"

I touched her hand. I sensed how upset she was. "Oh my gosh! That's terrible. Must have been quite a shock for you. Did you tell her?"

"No, I couldn't break her heart like that. He means the world to her. She loves him more than anyone else in the world but the next time I run into that conniving scoundrel, I'll tell him I know about his wandering ways and if he doesn't want Evie to know, he better cut it out."

I laughed. "That's the Mrs. Townsend I know, smart and not afraid to tell it like it is."

Mrs. Townsend smiled at my last remark. "You know Lana, there's nothing like the old-fashioned way of meeting a person through an introduction by a friend, at a church social, or neighborhood picnic. I have given up on all this internet dating stuff. You just don't know who's out there. So, when you start to date, please be careful, you're too precious a friend to lose. Always be safe."

I stood and gave her a big hug. "Don't worry. I'll always be careful."

She turned and left to go find a book. Since there was no one in my section presently, I removed the newspaper covering the designated page of that newest volume and snuck a peak. The page displayed a beautiful watercolor illustration of the Carnival Masked Ball painting that I read hung in The Doge's Palace. Women dressed in beautiful gemstone-colored gowns of emerald-green, ruby, and sapphire danced around the ballroom floor with escorts in formal matching waistcoats. They all wore colorful and creative masks to keep their identity a secret and celebrate the event.

As I took a closer look at the print, I noticed one couple stood in the center of the ballroom and did not wear masks to hide their faces. All the masked couples formed a semi- circle around them. Another couple had stepped forward to stand near the couple in the center. That gentleman was thin, dressed entirely in black, while his face was hidden by a scary black and white mask with an unsettling image of a protruding bird's beak, his companion wore a beautiful mask and looked stunning dressed in a sapphire blue gown with a ruffled neckline.

They along with the others applauded the unmasked couple. *What's this?* I pulled out a magnifying glass from my desk drawer to get a closer look. The man in the center bore an uncanny resemblance to Marco while his dance partner had long red curls and green dots for eyes. My jaw dropped so fast I thought it would hit my desk. I shot back down into my chair puzzled. Another coincidence or is my imagination getting the better of me? The caption under the drawing read, "The Doge's son Rinaldo and his dance partner step forward to watch Count Marcello Banelli and his lovely betrothed join the other guests for a dance at The Doge's Ball to celebrate the official opening of Carnival season."

I couldn't stop myself from looking at the other illustrations. One depicted a palatial ballroom with gold gilding and multi-colored Venetian glass chandeliers. I glanced at the two young couples dressed to the hilt and ready to dance. Something about both couples drew me in. I looked through my magnifying glass again to examine them further. The man in the center did bear a striking resemblance to my EMT and Marco. Odd, the thin son of the Doge was built like my mystery man in black. *Could it be or did I have too much wine last night?* Marcello's lady, his betrothed, had long red curls down to her waist and green dots for eyes. Her features, although an artist's rendering, bore more than a slight resemblance to me...and her dress was the emerald- green one from my dream. I gasped and had to cover my mouth afraid someone would think I was going mad.

I forced myself to read further even though I was at work. With this latest development, I couldn't wait for the library to close. Lucky for me, my section remained empty of patrons, so I scanned the next page. A quick reading revealed that Count Banelli was the best friend of the Doge's two sons, Rinaldo the oldest and Raymondo the youngest. Rinaldo was the one in black on the dance floor while Raymondo wore a deep purple royal brocade robe. In another illustration, Rinaldo's unmasked image was turned to face the happy couple. His profile revealed he had a long, thin, pointed nose like my mystery man. I further read The Doge had just announced the count's engagement causing the other dancers to surround them.

Not enough sleep? Too much wine? I was sure there was a reasonable explanation. I closed the book unable to assimilate everything I just saw. My mind spun with possible explanations. I glanced at my watch. Four o'clock...less than an hour until I meet Marco. Before I could finish that thought, I heard someone approaching. I looked up and saw that mystery man coming straight toward my desk again. He stared at me with his piercing black eyes.

"Madam," he bowed in his strange manner before continuing. "I'm sorry if I offended you earlier. It was impolite for me not to introduce myself. My name is pronounced Reeno, and I am hoping to meet an old friend here. His name is Marco and he's from Venice like I am. Have you seen him today?"

Venice? Why suddenly is everyone from Venice? I shook my head "no." For some inexplicable reason, call it women's intuition, I didn't trust him and decided to lie.

"I'm sorry, sir, but I don't know the person you're talking about. If someone comes to my desk with that name, I'll mention our conversation." He smiled. "You're so quick to answer, I believe you know more than you're letting on. I saw the two of you together at a local restaurant the other night and here in the library. But for now, I'll take back my question, but remember, I will be watching you."

He placed two fingers on his eyelids and moved them toward mine before he bowed, putting his front arm across his midriff, his other arm behind his back. "Thank you for your time. Have a good day."

With that, Reeno, as he called himself, turned and left. *How did he know about the restaurant? Was he the tall thin man in the shadows who stared at us?* I held onto my arms chilled by that last thought and grabbed the sweater over the back of my chair. He made me apprehensive to say the least. I must tell Marco about this curious man and his odd message.

I soon heard someone else approach my desk. *I hope it's not that Reeno again!* I paused, elated to see it was Marco. He was early. I breathed a sigh of relief. My knight in shining armor arrived just in time to protect me from that scary man. Strange, Marco was early today. He usually waits until I'm almost ready to close. Maybe he sensed I needed help.

I waved for him to approach my desk anxious to tell him about the peculiar man who was looking for him and to show him the print of the two people who resembled us. He stopped at the first book aisle and turned as soon as he saw me wave. I couldn't wait to tell him everything. When he arrived at my desk, I was so excited my voice became louder than a whisper. I blurted out what was on my mind, even though patrons began to fill my section.

"Marco, I'm so happy to see you. You can't imagine how much. I want to show you something and need to give you a message someone left for you as well."

Marco looked surprised. "You look upset. What is it darling? Is everything all right? Who would leave a message for me here? I'm so far from home."

I always wore my feelings on my sleeve. "A very strange man named Reeno has visited the library several times in the last few days. He's thin, wears unusual clothing, mostly black, and has a pointed nose. This morning, he claimed he knew you and wanted me to tell you he was here looking for you."

Marco didn't seem bothered by any of this. "Reeno? I don't recall anyone by that name." Marco answered easily, not visibly concerned by my information. I was more nervous about this strange man than he was. I caught my breath after telling him about Reeno and pointed to the large volume in the center of my desk. "I found this book on the floor next to my desk earlier. Please take a close look at the couple in the center of the drawing."

I turned the large volume around to face him. Marco studied the drawing but remained silent, almost stoic. I asked, "Don't you think it peculiar the couple without masks resembles us? Even more so, look at the man's name. It's very close to yours."

He shrugged his shoulders, I think trying to distract me, but that didn't stop me from continuing, "Look at the thin man in black. He sure looks like Reeno. Same distinctive nose and by coincidence his name in the book is Rinaldo."

Marco paused. "It's just coincidence, my darling, all pure coincidence. You're reading too much into that illustration which I might add is an abstract watercolor...abstract being the key word here. It's hard for me to distinguish the characters' precise facial features. Besides, in Venice, Banelli is a common name like how you say here Smith. So is Rinaldo for that matter but let me take a closer look. Please turn the page to face you."

I turned the book around and Marco walked behind my chair. He stroked my hair and leaned over my shoulder to get a closer look as he kissed the top of my head. A nearby patron looked over at us. "Hey, you two lovebirds, cut that out. No kissing. This is a public library." Everyone else nearby laughed.

I didn't find Marco's actions comical. "Marco, please stop. This is not appropriate. You could get me fired. Since nothing I've said sounds familiar, I don't know what to think." Marco lifted my face and looked into my eyes. "Remember I said I needed to talk to you?"

I nodded. "Yes, I do."

Marco whispered in my ear. "We need to go to a more private location so we can be alone."

Surprised he would even ask that while I was at work, I exclaimed. "You know that's impossible for me until after five. Why all this secrecy?" Marco remained silent but appeared anxious, so I repeated. "Marco, I'm at work. I can't just get up and leave. We can talk after the library closes besides there are too many people near us to talk now."

Marco shook his head. "No, we need to talk immediately. Maybe I can fix it so we can."

The curious or should I say nosey eyes and ears of the patrons near my desk remained focused on us. Embarrassed, I wanted them to stop listening and looking at us and wondered how he could fix that.

In a sudden move, Marco waved his hands in the air. Like magic, everyone in the room except for the two of us froze in place. They all looked like department store mannequins each with their own unique pose. I shook my head and blinked my eyes several times trying to clear that unbelievable image from my mind, but each time I opened my eyes the view remained the same.

Marco noticed my look of surprise and tried to reassure me. "It's all right my darling...I"

Stunned, I interrupted him before he could say any more. "How did you do that? You said we had to go somewhere private to talk. Are we leaving soon? Is that why you did that? Where are you taking me?"

Marco reached for my hand. "Please Lana, don't worry. I would never place you in harm's way. I love you more than life itself. We just need a little privacy to discuss the future."

The future? Is that his way of breaking up with me?

I sat back fearful of what I just witnessed and what he might say. Marco took a deep breath before he continued. "After we leave the library, everyone will return to normal but won't remember anything about what just happened or about our departure. One of the other librarians will come over and cover your desk as if she had been here all day. As for our talk, I have everything planned for us. So please calm down. I love you and sense how frightened you are."

A deep chill crept up my spine while my nerves lost control of my shivering body. I started to cry. "Once we leave here? What do you mean you have everything planned for us?"

He kissed the top of my head. "Please trust me. We will be fine." He placed his hands on my shoulders and glanced down at the page again. I loved the feel of his touch, but this time it frightened me as much as it aroused me.

Marco kissed my cheek. "Please don't be so afraid. You

know how much I love you. When I touch you, I can feel how stressed you."

Still standing behind me, he looked at that illustration once more I'm sure trying to distract me and added. "Hmm...you may be right. The more I look at that page, the more that couple does resemble us. While I'm here behind you. Please stand and close your eyes. I have a big surprise for you."

I realized no one could see us because of his unexpected magic trick. The element of surprise added more stress to my already taxed brain. "But I'm still on duty, Marco." He rubbed my shoulders. "Remember no one can see us so please do as I ask. No more questions or you'll ruin my surprise."

"Surprise?" I blurted out as my mind told me to get out of there as fast as I could. "What about all these people just frozen in place? You frighten me so much I don't think I want your surprise."

Marco reassured me. "But it's the one I've promised. Please stand close to the book and when I tell you open your eyes."

To this day, I don't understand why, maybe because I was in love with him, but I did as he asked. I stood and Marco instructed, "Okay my love, please leave the book on that page and open your eyes."

What just happened? Do my eyes deceive me? As I looked down at the open page, I trembled with fear wondering if all this was all a dream or a nightmare. The page content had changed. The illustration of the Carnival Ball had vanished. The gold leaf border remained but what appeared to be a deep dark hole expanded and replaced both the text and the picture. Before I could ask any more questions, Marco placed one of his arms around my waist, grabbed my hand, and leaned us forward. I gasped, unable to grasp what was happening. As soon as we leaned forward, that black hole became so large, it covered the floor around my desk and kept expanding until it became big enough for both of us to fit through. Marco looked up at the ceiling and called out. "Othero, we're ready to Travel. Send for us at once!"

Othero? Aurellia mentioned Othero but why was Marco calling out to him? My lover then gave me a slight tug. I held my breath as together we fell forward into that deep dark hole. I was so frightened, I couldn't speak, couldn't even scream. Only air came out of my mouth while my heart pounded like steel drums. Finally, when I could yell out for help, no one answered, no one heard me. I was scared out of my mind. By this point, I needed assurance and fast; I squeezed Marco's hand so tight my hand hurt. I looked at him terrified, while he remained as cool as a cucumber, like he had done this before.

At first, we fell straight down into that black hole. The black void surrounded us. After a few more minutes, the hole's fast-moving circular air made our bodies spin while we kept holding hands. We continued to spin around so fast, I was amazed I didn't become dizzy. Clenching my eyes shut, I opened them only after Marco had steadied our descent. Our spinning slowed the lower we fell.

Once our descent stabilized, I opened my eyes to see people from different eras in history appear like spirits, their clothing and hair blowing in the winds of time. They came close enough to touch us and reached out with their pale ghostly arms, but we descended so fast it was too difficult for them to catch us.

As we dropped deeper and deeper into what I perceived were different centuries, the ghostlike figures and clothing changed with each long drop. First, I saw women in modern dress. Their skirt length changed from short to mid-length then as flappers short again. From there, they wore floor length dresses and ball gowns while the men went from different styles of suits and ties to more formal attire and waistcoats. Since my journey rivaled a tour of a fashion museum, my curiosity lessened my fear.

As we passed by each era, I realized we must be traveling

back in time. *Could that be? I read about Time Travel but never dreamed it could happen in real life, especially mine. Still, I kept hoping this entire episode was just another one of my unusual dreams.*

Suddenly, our pace quickened, spinning us around and around again like tops. I panicked when I looked down to see we were heading for a crash landing on what appeared to be a hard surface, a stone floor, near some large body of blue green water.

I screamed, "Marco help! If we don't slow down, we're going to die!" I began to cry but Marco remained calm the entire time and squeezed my hands for comfort. I closed my eyes as tight as I could. We approached that stone floor at the highest speed imaginable, but to my surprise we landed unscathed. The stones felt as soft as a cotton cloud and cushioned our fall.

Sitting up, I felt the coolness of the marble floor tiles against my legs. I found it hard to believe that neither one of us was hurt. I looked around trying to discern where we were, but from where I sat, a stone wall blocked my view.

Marco stood up and dusted himself off. "Please Lana, allow me to help you stand. We must rid ourselves of the Travel Dust before others who wish me harm know we Travelled."

Others who wish him harm? Why didn't he mention them before?

Marco helped me to my feet, and I, too, brushed the heavy travel dust off my clothes. Looking through the enormous open arch in front of us, I saw it was daylight, and we were standing on a curved balcony overlooking a busy waterway below.

Marco took my hand and led me inside through a doorway which had colorful stained-glass windows on either side. The sun's rays enhanced the beauty of the window's floral designs in reds, yellows, and royal blues. Still shaken from our unusual method of Travel, I looked around trying to figure out where we were. We had entered a massive room with fieldstone walls and high ceilings. Large colorful coats of arms lined the walls as did swords and shields. My new surroundings resembled that of a castle or perhaps a royal manor house.

Marco pulled on a long rope chain with a brass bell on the end of it. Anxious, I turned when I heard someone enter the room. A beautiful female attendant dressed in a blue and white striped uniform with a floor length skirt entered. She curtsied. I noticed she wore her waist length black hair braided behind her. She glanced at Marco with her large brown eyes obviously happy to see him and, oddly enough, spoke in proper British English but with a hint of an Italian accent like Marco's.

"Welcome back, Count Banelli, from your business trip. Your staff missed you. If there is anything you and your guest needs, please let us know and we will take care of everything at once."

Marco bowed. "Thank you, Sophia. I'll need a room for Miss Lana and we'll both need something to eat. We had a long journey back home. Anything Gracia chooses for our dinner will be appreciated."

Count Banelli? Are we in his palazzo?

Marco turned to me. "Sophia as well as many others in my household staff learned to speak English because we in Venice do a great deal of business with ambassadors from the British Empire and often welcome them into our homes."

Sophia smiled, appreciative of his introduction. "Thank you for your kind comment, my Count. I work hard and hope I please you." When she turned to me, however, she shot me such an icy stare, ice crystals could have formed in the air between us. Her disdain for my visit was written all over her face. After another quick look, she sneered at my short skirt which I'm sure added to her disapproval. My curiosity got the better of me. I forgot about Sophia's unspoken opinion of me and asked. "Marco, where are we?"

Marco dismissed Sofia and made sure we were alone before he answered. He waved his arm around in the air to show me this magnificent room. "Welcome to my Venetian palazzo. Palazzo Banelli. We are in 1588 and your thoughts about the illustration in that book were correct. That was us."

His palazzo? 1588? Us? At the Carnival Ball? How could that be?

I was so tongue tied I had to pinch my arm as hard as I could to make sure I was awake. My arm hurt so I knew I had heard him correctly and this was all real. My perplexed expression must have said it all because Marco walked over and caressed me. I placed my head on his shoulder for comfort before getting up enough courage to ask what was really on my mind.

"Are you the real Count Banelli? The one mentioned in that large history book. How did we end up in 1588 and why did you take me here? Are there people who really want to harm you? It's because of the treasure, isn't it?"

Marco smiled as he kissed my cheek. "Yes, Lana, I am the real Count Banelli. Please calm down. You'll only make yourself sick if you don't. Yes, there are individuals who wish me harm, but as I already told you no one will hurt you if I am with you. I alone have the treasure they want and do not want you privy to where it is. Please, come and sit with me on the balcony where I will answer all your questions."

Marco took my hand and walked me back out to the curved balcony. To my surprise, it overlooked the Grand Canal of Venice. Worrying more about our safety, I was in shock when we landed and had failed to take in the city's unique ambiance. I ran over to the stone boundary so I could scan every inch of this remarkable view. The sea breeze cooled my flushed face while my view soaked in the blue-green waters filled with gondolas of all sizes and colors. Marco came over and stood next to me. He whispered in my ear. "To me, this is the most beautiful scenery in the world."

He reached for my hand and kissed it. "Come let's sit." He took my hand and led us away from the view to a curved stone bench where we both sat. I still couldn't believe what just happened. Here I was in Venice, the city of my dreams, with the love of my life looking through the enormous arched window in front of us at the busy Grand Canal. I was so amazed that at this point, Marco could have told me he was a serial killer, and I would be fine with that. I always wanted to visit Venice, but must admit, I never thought Time Travel would be my way of getting here.

Still in a bit of shock, I stood and left Marco sitting on the bench to peer over the edge of the balcony. I wanted to soak in the canal view one more time. Gondolas, service boats, even a shiny black wedding gondola decorated with fresh white and pink flowers and a singing gondolier passed underneath us. My mind snapped back when Marco's comments woke me from my wonderful reverie. "Lana, I hope you're not upset with me for taking you here. I couldn't bear the thought of living without you. I love you."

"And I love you. I'm not upset at all. Trust me, I'm as surprised as you by my feelings and still amazed by our method of Travel. If this was the surprise you promised, it was the most wonderful one I've ever had. Venice is as beautiful and unique as I imagined. I've seen photos but only of modern Venice. Where we are is the original city, the old city."

Marco smiled to let me know he was pleased with my answer. He walked over and placed his arm around my waist. I kissed his cheek. "Yes, Lana, this is the city written about in history books known as The Venetian Republic. I wanted you to experience it the way I live it and love it. You wonder how we managed to Travel back to my time. There are a few very talented wizards in Venice, and I am lucky to have one named

Othero in my fold. Othero helped me find you and Travel to your time.

"You'll know more about my past very soon. Before I Traveled to you, Othero instructed me on his Rules of Travel. He told me that because of what happened to me in that deadly duel, I would have to start my journey as the Shadow Person my body had become. Once I found my designated location, and what I had come for, I would become visible in human form but remain a Time Traveler. I would return to being human again only after I completed my assigned task of obtaining the key to unlock my family's treasure. When and if that happens, I will have to call out to Othero by name and instruct him of my success."

Shadow Person? Marco was my vision. And a Time Traveler? Aurellia's explanations were spot on.

My head began to throb. My face burned like it was on fire because I found it difficult to wrap my thoughts around what he just revealed. Marco continued. "After researching the treasure for some time, I asked Othero to locate that special key and send me there to acquire it. Little did I know when I found you wearing the key I found a second more valuable treasure, that of our love."

Wearing the key? My pendant? He wants my pendant.

He leaned over and kissed my cheek before he resumed. "I journeyed to the future to lay claim to my family's legacy. Once I found it, my heart wouldn't allow me to steal it and leave you behind. Lana, you mean more to me than life itself."

Tears of joy filled my eyes as he continued. "If you trust me, we can claim the treasure together and find happiness for the rest of our lives. Please, come and sit next to me. Listen as I tell you the treasure's real story."

CHAPTER
SEVEN

followed Marco back to that stone bench and sat down next to him eager to learn as much as possible about my mystery lover and the history of my locket. Funny, I was so taken by my new surroundings and Marco's love that I wasn't concerned about how and if I would get home. All I wanted was to spend as much time as possible with him. He flashed another one of his irresistible smiles as he began to tell me his story.

"We are in my present, 1588. I *am* Count Marcello Banelli, the same person in those history books you discovered on your desk. This is my family palazzo and my home. I never lied to you about my name. 'Marco' is an endearing shorter version of Marcello that my mother liked to call me. My parents died when I was young, five to be precise, from a disease a deadly plague that swept through most of our city. I escaped their fate because my mother sent me by royal coach to live with her sister, my Aunt Linda in Rome. That's why the story about your own family's deaths tugged at my heart. Anyway, when I returned to Venice, six years later, I went to live with my grandparents who raised me to be an honorable man and whom I loved with all my heart.

"Eight years after my parents died, my grandmother passed

away from the ailments of old age. Of course, I was devastated. I felt like I had lost two mothers. I know, especially after your accident, you realize how hard something like that hits you."

I thought about my own loss and realized how deeply he mourned as well. That's why he was so sensitive to my needs. I focused again on Marco's story.

"It was just Grandfather and me along with a group of loyal and caring servants. I was the center of his attention. We spent a great deal of time together, and, when I got older, he instructed me on the duties and the historical significance of my royal title. I watched him run his household like an oiled clock with all the servants, gardeners, and kitchen staff, and in observing him, I learned how to do it. He always reminded me to treat the servants with kindness, be honest with them, and generous to them for their efforts. My grandfather was in the best of health for his age up until last year, when he took ill and passed away. I sat by his bedside hoping his illness would take a turn for the better, but alas that didn't happen. When he knew he was dying, he asked everyone except for me to leave his bedroom. With his dying breath, he confided in me that my ancestor Sergio Casselli buried the treasure somewhere in this palazzo and it was my duty to our family lineage to find that box along with the key which opens it.

"Grandfather made me vow never to destroy the fruitwood box painted by Raphael in my efforts to open it. I gave him my word I would not do so in his honor. I looked over at him as he closed his eyes, took his last breath, and died with the peace of mind that I pledged to do what he asked. Since my word is my bond, I must make that happen in his memory."

I held Marco's hand, realizing he had been through as much heartbreak as I. He wiped a tear from the corner of his eye and cleared his throat.

"I will tell you how I found you. I realized when I was still in my shadow form that I needed help honoring my pledge to

Grandfather. My wizard Othero studied his crystal ball for days on end before he advised my spirit that my path to the key lies within my own family history.

"He discovered you while searching for the key in his crystal ball and sent me to you as a Shadow Person. Once I Travelled to your time and place, Othero kept me hovering near you and the library for months."

Within his own family history? What did he mean by that? I wanted to learn more, so I didn't interrupt.

"Othero soon advised me he located a future relative of the Councilman's betrothed, Contessa Marchesa Genolli. She was engaged to my great-grandfather Sergio Casselli on my mother's side hence the different last name. He hoped to keep the treasure for their own future by having the key made into a piece of exquisite jewelry, a pendant, which he gave Marchesa as an engagement gift. If one closely inspects the pendant, a small gold lip is hidden under the border of diamonds which serves as the key. Marchesa kept the pendant with The Doge's blessing after the young couple was forced to break up because of a power dispute between the two families. Not long after that Marchesa had to leave Venice."

Marchesa Genolli? How is this story possible? She's my relative! For some inexplicable reason, I ran my trembling finger under the gem lined border of my pendant. *What's this? Ouch.* That lip stuck into my fingertip. Distracted by my locket, I tried to focus again on Marco's story.

"Marchesa was not only beautiful but a student of the arts, savvy in the ways of business in her time, and a dedicated animal lover. After dinner, I will show you her portrait in the grand hallway. Anyway, when she realized she would no longer be entitled to any of our estate, she was smart enough to know she would remain in control of some of it for as long as she possessed that key.

"A few years passed before Marchesa left Venice unannounced. Her uncle was in the shipping business and after she confided in him that her life and those of her husband and children were at risk, he offered to help them. He placed Marchesa and her children on a ship headed to La Florida. Her husband followed on another ship. Of course, since she always wore the pendant, she took the key with her. She knew that if she safeguarded the key, either the Banelli family would have to pay her a hefty ransom to get it back or by passing down the key to her heirs, she would keep the treasure safe for them. Before she died, she took the pendant and chain off her neck and gave it to her eldest daughter. In her dying wish, she stated she wanted her legacy to be that the necklace be given to the eldest daughter of each generation."

That's why my mother gave it to me. I'm her eldest daughter.

"The key vanished soon after Marchesa's death. No one laid public claim to its ownership, so we assumed someone in Marchesa's family kept it hidden. The pendant had a unique shape, a hexagon with one large garnet at its center surrounded by small diamonds. As I said, there was a small hook under the bottom of the pendant that, when pulled out, served as the actual key. Even without the key, my great grandfather had the forethought to protect the box as a worthy treasure in and of itself so the responsibility for finding both treasures now rests with me."

I looked at my pendant, aware that it matched Marco's description. Marco stared at it as well. Marco moved closer to me. "May I hold your pendant so I might look at the workmanship and admire its beauty?'

I nodded and held my locket up by its chain just like I did for Aurellia. He held the pendant in his hand, "Beautiful. It's as exquisite as you are."

He returned the pendant to my hand. Pressing it tight in my palm, I listened to more of his story. "My grandfather claimed my great grandfather, the Doge's Chief Council, hid the crown somewhere in this palazzo before he died.

"I know what you're thinking. Finding the treasure is like finding a tiny piece of glass in the canal, but after Grandfather's death, my lifelong mission has become to locate that key and keep my promise to him."

My fingers ran down his cheek until they touched his lips. "You're a loyal and loving grandson. Your grandfather would be proud." He kissed my fingertips.

"Trust me, Lana, I combed every passageway of this palazzo even finding secret ones I never knew existed. I hung from a thick beam like a carnival artist attempting to look under one of the support beams over the canal. That was a tricky feat even for a young man as agile as I am but nevertheless, I found nothing there. I couldn't find it anywhere I searched. I became discouraged thinking I should give up until one night I was desperate and called out to my grandfather's spirit to send me a sign. I tossed and turned, worried I might not be able to keep my promise. Trying to clear my mind, I lit the gas lamp on my nightstand and stared at the ceiling. I scanned every inch of the ceiling hoping an idea would come to me, besides staring at all that blank space might help me fall asleep. But instead, one corner of the ceiling caught my eye. The plaster was peeling and crumbling from that corner. Could that be the sign from my grandfather? Foolish thinking I thought."

Reassuring him, I interjected. "No Marco. I believed spirits can communicate with loved ones. There are days I hear my mother's voice whispering in my ear."

Marco pulled me over for a quick kiss. He looked into my eyes as he continued. "I heard creaking noises from above as well and needed to know why, so for safety I took a sharp knife out of my nightstand drawer, got out of bed, and lit the small gas lamp next to my bed to take with me. Was someone up there? If so, what were they doing?

"I tried to be as quiet as possible. If my great grandfather did hide the treasure up there, I hoped not to tip my hand. I closed my bedroom door, walked over to the attic stairway behind a plain wooden door, and climbed the one tall flight of stairs leading to the attic. I was as quiet as a church mouse aware that I might not be alone up there.

"Once in the attic, I didn't see or hear anything or anyone. It was dark, my light dim. I paid little attention to where I was walking. My foot stumbled on something solid built into the side of one of the ceiling beams and hidden by wood scrapings. I positioned my lamp on the floor so its light would focus on that beam. Wiping the wood scraps aside, I pulled off the added wood panels and found that beam to be hollow.

"I don't need to tell you how surprised I was to find a thin burlap sack protecting a rectangular object hidden inside that beam. Excited, I hoped it was the treasure. If it was, I reminded myself to take extra precautions not to fall or drop the object after I pulled it out from the sack. Once I removed it safely, I was astonished to look at the very object Grandfather had described to me.

"Since the box was not heavy and had an ornate metal handle made of sterling silver on the front side, I placed the thin burlap bag in my pocket and decided to carry it by its handle down to my room. When sunlight broke through the cracks in the roof, I blew out my lamp and left it there since I couldn't carry both down those narrow stairs. I kept checking behind me to make sure no one watched or followed. As I have already told you, many people wanted to claim this treasure.

"Once in the safety of my room, I placed the box on my small desk. The morning sun entering through the window over my desk gave me enough light to inspect the box more closely. It was more magnificent than I had ever imagined. The chest was made of polished fruitwood and painted with a very intricate, detailed design. A wedding scene with a floral border of lilies dominated its lid while a sterling silver lock was fixed to the front of the chest. I studied the unique shape of the lock and realized it needed to be opened with an equally unusual key. The only way for me to confirm if this box contained my family's treasure was to find that specific key and open the box. Until I could do that, I removed some floorboards near but not under my bed and hid the box there for safety.

"Tired, I lay down elated by my find but so exhausted from my search that I soon drifted into a deep but restless sleep. I dreamt my beloved grandmother's spirit came to me. Beautiful as in life, she hugged me. 'Marcello, I'll always love you and protect you, but I'm concerned for your safety. That's why I came to you.' When she let go, she warned me in the most serious voice to keep a watchful eye on everything and everyone around me. I can still hear her speak those words. 'My beloved grandson, be aware. Stay alert. Please take nothing or anyone for granted. Watch yourself in everything you do and everyone you meet because someone you know well, and trust wishes to harm you. I will be watching over you and sending all my spiritual protection.' She then smiled a most angelic smile. 'I can see what the future holds for you and know you will find your true love in a distant place. She will be the one who will give you the key.'"

I took a deep breath trying to absorb all that he just told me. I've watched movies with less intrigue. Marco focused on my pendant again. I knew he was trying to ask me something. Tears flooded my eyes. I wanted to ask him if my locket was the true reason for his attention, but before I could, he continued.

"Before I tell you any more about the key, I must reveal the true nature of my being to you. I'm a spirit having died a few days after I discovered the location of that box in 1588. We have Traveled back to four days before my death. That's why my servants can see me. They would not be able if I remained in that shadow state.

"My grandmother was right. I should have heeded her warning. My safety was at risk. Two people wanted to kill me for that treasure but even after they did, they were unable to find it. I called out to Othero to help me. He kept my spirit alive and hovering nearby. He knew my spirit would remain in transition until I fulfilled my promise to my grandfather. At that point in time, Othero was the only one who could see or hear me. My spirit remained strong because he gave me hope that I would find the key. I am what Aurellia referred to as a Shadow Person. She told you the truth. My soul cannot find peace until my pledge is kept.

"Aurellia is a special mystic because she can communicate with Shadow People. She helps those of us in a state of flux find peace. My transition to a ghost or a future with you will come only after I keep my word and lay claim to the treasure for my future heirs. I wish I knew what the future held for me, for us, but that's a chance I must take."

That's why she said not to be afraid of him, but now that I've fallen in love with him, I find that I could lose him. My already shattered heart couldn't bear another loss that significant.

Marco continued but sensed my mind was wandering. "Lana, are you well?"

I nodded trying to redirect my thoughts back to his story.

"All right then, I'll continue. Othero searched his crystal ball until he found the precise geographic location of the key. Needing an experienced spiritualist from that area, he contacted Aurellia.

I agreed to let him send my shadow to her. Once I found her, I found you and appeared to you as that shadow every time you blinked your eyes for months. I hoped to steal the key while you slept but that became impossible. I couldn't let myself betray your trust because I fell in love with you.

"Othero reminded me, 'Marcello you must keep that promise to your grandfather. Take that locket by any means possible even if it means harming the one who wears it.' That's why my shadow followed you at first to keep an eye on the key and prevent anyone else who may have followed from taking it.

"Lana, please believe me, I do love you with all my heart. You asked if I was at the scene of your tragic accident. Yes, Aurellia called on my spirit at the exact time of the accident. As we watched what was unfolding through her crystal ball, she turned to me. 'Lana needs our help if we wish to save her life and retrieve her necklace.' Aurellia waved her large slender hands over her crystal ball and used her magnetic energy to zap my spirit.

'Go Marco, be brave. Save Lana and save that necklace. Go now, we may not have another opportunity to do this even with all the magic in the universe.'

"With one sudden spell, she diverted me to be by your side. My spirit dove immediately into your car, stopped you from hitting your head, and protected you from death. You were still unconscious, but I knew I had to get you out of that car, so I carried you to an empty ambulance. As I did, I heard Aurellia's voice in my ear. 'You'll scare her if you confront her as a spirit. I must change that right now. Hold on tight.'

"Once we were safely inside the ambulance, I heard Aurellia whisper an incantation and snap her fingers. I felt hot and shaky but when I looked down, I first saw my legs appear in the flesh. My true nature, my true body then appeared temporarily just as it was before I was murdered. I held your head and stroked your cold face.

"My care helped you become conscious again. You saw me in my human form first. I stayed with you until you fell asleep. I watched over you then and have been ever since. You see, we share strong family connections that go back to Venice. When I heard Aurellia snap her fingers again, I knew she wanted my spirit to return with your necklace, but I loved you too much to steal it from you. I returned to her in my temporary human form because she couldn't find a way to reverse the spell. When she realized I didn't steal your necklace, she contacted Othero for another plan. You can only imagine how disappointed he was."

I was so stunned, I couldn't speak. My body felt weak and frozen at the same time as if I was paralyzed. My stomach churned. My mind mused. *That's just my luck. I find the man of my dreams and he's a shadow. Was a Shadow Person even capable of love? Could I believe he really loved me, or had he pursued me just to get that key?*

After he finished, I became concerned about my feelings and our future together. As always, I blurted out what was on my mind. "Marco, please tell me our love is not a sham. Assure me that if I give you my pendant, you'll not leave me, die, or vanish forever?"

He remained silent and turned from my gaze to look out over the Grand Canal. As he did, my mind reviewed every instance of when I saw his shadow. Funny, I haven't seen that shadow since I met Marco in the flesh. How stupid of me. Why didn't I connect the dots? I was so in love, my subconscious refused.

Marco stared into my eyes again. "I hope with all my heart that I'll return to you. The risks are great, but I must take them to keep my pledge. Even after my promise is fulfilled, my shadow could turn into a ghost and never be a living person again. I have no control over that. Othero believes that will not happen because your love has given me so much to live for. Nevertheless, since I gave my word of honor to my grandfather, I must proceed."

He squeezed my hand. "For this moment, let's think happy thoughts only. I want to share my city, my home, and my customs with you. You look lovely but people will stare unless you dress in the fashion of my time. Come let's go back inside."

My thoughts were in a tailspin from all this latest information. Is this another of my unusual dreams? It must be. Marco was too good to be true. I pinched my arm again. It hurt and we were both still here. Dazed by all of this, I staggered a bit as we walked back inside. Marco held onto me tight as he approached the bell and pulled the thick gold braided rope attached to it. After a few minutes, Sofia returned, and Marco instructed her.

"Sofia, you have already met our guest, Lady Lana. Please take her to one of the royal guest rooms, fill her tub with rose petals and warm water so she can relax from her long journey, and then find her suitable clothes."

Sofia nodded affirmatively to Marco but looked at me disgusted. She curtseyed. I sensed she still was not happy about my visit. She glared at my short skirt and stared at my make-up before advising me. "Of course, I will do as my count asks and try to make you look presentable. Come with me."

She took my hand and led me out of the room and into a long corridor. From our previous encounter, although brief, I could tell that besides being beautiful with long black hair, a light complexion, and penetrating dark brown eyes, she was well educated, speaking multiple languages, took pride in her service, and was always loyal to her count's wishes.

The rest of the way, she remained quiet and refused to speak to me unless necessary, something I found very odd, but every now and then she would cast me a disparaging look. She did manage to utter a "follow me" as she led me down a second long hallway filled with more suits of armor, crossed swords on the walls, as well as tapestries of colorful Venetian gardens and the Grand Canal. There were so many things to see, my eyes couldn't absorb them all. History has always been my passion, and now I find myself walking through a living museum. In such awe of the beauty and art of my surroundings, I forgot to be afraid.

We walked by one flight of stairs and then further down that hallway until we passed by two brightly painted doorways, one in green and the other in lavender. I spotted a third door in a robin's egg blue. That door was the charm because Sofia, still silent, motioned for me to follow as she unlocked it. When I stepped inside, my mind couldn't believe all the beauty I witnessed. I stood in the middle of a bedroom fit for a princess with gold gilded furniture, a high bed with a brocade canopy and footstool, and detailed paintings of colorful Venetian scenes painted and signed by Italian Masters. I turned completely around so many times I became dizzy trying to study and absorb every nook and cranny of my remarkable surroundings. "These walls hold an art collection as impressive as any art museum. I can't believe I'm standing amidst works by Italian masters."

Sofia still was curt. "My count is an art lover as were his parents."

I didn't know how to make her warm up to me. I wished her no harm and was certainly not a threat unless she had secret feelings for Marco. Sofia then waved for me to follow her past the bed to an opening with luxurious windows that faced the Canal. I blurted out as soon as I saw the tub, "This is the most elegant bedroom suite I have ever seen. It's impressive enough for a royal guest and that shiny copper bathtub could easily fit two."

Unimpressed, she at once instructed me. "My lady, please go back and wait on the bed as we prepare your bath. Please disrobe. I left a dressing gown for you on the bed. Because my count asked me to do this for you, I planned and have arranged for help to heat your bath water and pour it into the tub. As we speak, the water heats in a large vat over this room's fireplace."

I undressed and took my shoes off my aching feet. I rubbed my numb toes awake from all the stress of Travel before I heard a gentle knock. I replied. "Please come in." When the bedroom door opened, three young girls in floral patterned uniforms and wearing heavy gloves entered carrying empty buckets to fill with the water heating in the large vat hanging in the bedroom's fireplace. I watched them work amazed at how such petite girls could lift such heavy buckets. They used a large ladle to place the hot water from the vat over the fireplace into their buckets before carrying them back and forth until they filled the tub. When they had finished, Sofia followed them to sprinkle rose petals and lavender in my bath water before dismissing them. She turned to me, still not smiling "My Lady, you will smell as lovely as the flowers that grace our garden."

She helped me take off my robe and I sat in the most luxurious bath of my life. My body absorbed the hot water. My nose inhaled the gentle floral fragrances coming from its steam. I took a deep breath. These sensations relieved my stress from our Travel and made me feel like I was in a grand European spa. *Could heaven be any better than this?*

Wanting to look my best for Marco, I soaked my body as Sofia washed my hair. A sudden sadness penetrated my heart as I wondered how short our time together would be. Tears flowed down my cheeks from that thought.

Sofia saw my tears but still appeared indifferent. She made me feel like I was just a job to her. She gently dried my hair with a large towel after my shampoo and added in a matter-of-fact tone, "My lady, this is no time for sad thoughts. You will soon be with the most desirable count in Venice. Every woman will envy you. Come, let's get you dry."

She then helped me out of the tub and wrapped an enormous soft cotton towel around me. We sat on the bed, and she finished drying my hair with smaller towels. Once finished, she stood and announced. "Please stay seated. I'll be right back with a most lovely surprise."

She left the room for a few minutes, returning with what looked like a long gown covered by a linen sack and emitting the fragrance of lavender. When she uncovered the gown, I saw the most exquisite deep violet satin gown, the color of an iris, with a ruffled bodice. Sophia hung it on a hook on the closet door before she sat next to me on the bed again and brushed and curled my hair. I stared in awe at that lovely gown, never having worn anything so elegant in my entire life. I was in such wonderment I almost missed what Sofia had to say.

"You're a lucky woman because my count requests your presence at dinner tonight. Dinners in our palazzo are formal. When you're ready, my lady, I will help you dress. I don't know your origin or why you appeared in that awful outfit for that matter, but I'm sure my count will want you to look like a royal Venetian lady suitable of his company and of our palazzo."

"My appearance must have shocked you, but I assure you it's normal at home. This gown is so beautiful, how did you attain it so quickly?" I responded.

Sofia shrugged her shoulders. "That is a seamstress's secret. We do use our talents to make sartorial magic happen every now and then. The deep color suits you. I had to estimate your size and select a gown that would fit you. Since I also serve as the palazzo's tailor, my guess should prove to be accurate. Are you ready to try it on?"

Still admiring that gorgeous evening gown with its layers of ruffles on the skirt and across the shoulders, I was more than happy to oblige. I stood and dropped my bath towel, so Sophia could help me get into the complicated undergarments. Once I had them on, I sat back down on the bed, and she styled my hair placing lavender rosettes on either side of my face. I then slipped into that beautiful gown. She took one look at me. "My lady, you look just like a royal Venetian lady."

I walked over to the floor length mirror and peeked at my transformation. Sofia had worked her magic, as she called it, turning me, a mousey librarian, into a royal lady of her time. I couldn't stop looking at myself and gasped. "I don't know what to say. You turned a mouse into a peacock."

Sofia nodded. "I appreciate that my efforts please you. If

they did not, I would not be doing my job. Are you ready to go to dinner?" I nodded and left my stance in front of the mirror. Sofia took my hand and led me through the hallway to the long formal dining room. I spotted Marco sitting at the head of a polished, oblong, wooden dining table with two large silver candelabras with rose-colored crystal drops placed at either end. He stood when I entered. Sofia remained silent and still refused to smile as she escorted me to the seat next to his. She turned quickly to leave before he greeted me by taking my hand and kissing it.

"Welcome Lana, you look exquisite. My palazzo pales to your beauty. Tonight, we shall enjoy a traditional Venetian dinner."

"Thank you. I'm very excited to be here." I replied as I took in the beauty of my surroundings. I felt like a tourist. Two huge Venetian glass chandeliers, their lights shaped like open orchids in blue, yellow, and lavender, held lit candles and hung above each end of the table. The lofty ceilings were painted to look like marble while two large tapestries depicting the many different gondolas on the Grand Canal graced the room's stone walls.

Marco smiled and broke my thoughts. "Lana, you are as lovely as a dream. By your expressions, I can see you like my ancestor's decorating skills."

He held my chair for me. I sat down on one of the tapestry high back chairs. "We will share a delicious dinner and afterwards, I will show you my grandmother's portrait and reveal more about how my dream of her led me to you."

Marco's butler dressed in an elegant black and white uniform entered the dining room through a side door. He carried a tall, red crystal decanter filled with white wine. After filling our gold lipped glasses, he proceeded to leave the decanter next to Marco and lit both candelabras.

"Thank you, Arturo. Please advise Gracia we are ready for dinner."

When the side door opened again, Gracia, an older woman with her graying brown hair tied up in a neat bun, entered carrying two bowls of soup on a large silver tray. As she passed, the soup's aroma wafted through the air. It smelled so good, my empty stomach growled. She put a bowl down in front of each of us, curtseyed, and left. The tomato-based chowder with halibut was most delicious. I have never tasted anything like it before. Marco noticed how I wolfed it down. I loved it so much I could have licked the bowl clean.

"Lana. I'm pleased you like our seafood, but savor it slowly," he laughed. "There's much more to come."

Gracia's timing was impeccable. She sent her young assistant to pick up our bowls as soon as we finished the last drops of our soup. Our second course was a pasta dish consisting of angel hair pasta in a marinara sauce with whole clams. Served in a large powder blue and cream porcelain bowl, it was fit for a queen. I flushed with embarrassment remembering Marco dining on my red and white mismatched plates I bought in a local thrift shop. I wondered what he thought of how I lived.

Gracia served us the pasta from a China platter and presented each of us with a gold fork and a knife, a far cry from my thin, mismatched stainless. After she left, Marco twirled the pasta on his fork with ease. He closed his eyes after tasting the first forkful.

"Forgive me for being so rude. I couldn't help myself. This dish is so flavorful. It's my grandmother's recipe and my favorite. Gracia made sure she followed my Nona's exact recipe. I missed having it while I Travelled. As you can see, we Venetians are noted for our seafood, fresh from our back door."

I followed suit by twirling the sauce covered pasta with my fork.

The homemade pasta soaked in the tangy seafood sauce felt like velvet in my mouth. This dish was so tasty I had seconds and ate too much. I didn't know about the multi courses of Italian dinners and was surprised when I learned we had not finished yet. I watched Gracia serve the third course of roast lamb and potatoes followed by a fresh green salad with olive oil and vinegar and finally fruits and nuts. I sat back holding my stomach filled with the most delicious meal of my life. Marco glanced at me and grinned at my discomfort.

"Gracia is a wonderful cook. Don't you think? We'll walk off this amazing dinner in a few minutes, but first I must ask if you would accompany me to The Doges' Carnival Ball tomorrow evening. The Doge's Ball is the premier social event of the season. I'd love to be your escort. We could dance until early morning just like that couple in the book."

I didn't know what to say. I was honored and surprised at the same time but unsure of how to respond without making a complete fool of myself. When I tried to answer, my mouth felt like it had been stuffed with cotton. I thought my wall flower persona wouldn't know the proper way to act in such high society let alone the fact that I knew nothing about the formal dancing of his time. I avoided looking at him so I wouldn't have to answer, but he wouldn't give up.

Marco winked, trying to make me smile. "Think about it. I won't force you, but I would be honored to have you accompany me. Besides, I bet I can read your mind." He touched the tip of my nose with his finger. "Yes, I was the one who sent those books. They are from my private library here."

Why wasn't I surprised? Marco explained. "I hoped they would help you discover more about my time, my culture, and of course the treasure. The Ball is our cultural treasure, a remarkable event, and the most romantic evening of the year."

After an aperitif, Marco didn't push me any further for a response. "Lana, come let me show you my grandmother's portrait. Would you like to learn more about her?"

I stood. "Of course I would." I was hungry to know more about her, along with that mysterious hand painted box, and my locket's odd-shaped key. He led us out of the dining room and down the long grand hallway. My eyes couldn't stop staring at the walls. Surrounded by so many formal portraits, we stopped under one of a bejeweled older woman, Marco beamed with pride as he pointed to her image.

"Lana, I'd like to introduce my Nona to you."

I studied her portrait. Speechless at first, I could see Marco bore a strong resemblance to her. She possessed long, black, curly hair sprinkled with gray and appeared to be in her sixties at the time of this portrait. She looked regal wearing a royal blue satin gown with a sapphire and diamond crown and necklace to match. With her fine features, light brown eyes like my lover's, and a robust complexion, she was indeed breathtaking. Marco directed my attention to her again.

"There she is, my beautiful Nona. I loved her beyond words. She never lied to me. That's why I should have trusted her in my dream."

We stood there for a few minutes holding hands before his eyes switched from the painting to my pendant. I covered it with my hand still hoping he wouldn't ask for it since it's the last memory I had from my mother. I directed my comments to the portrait again. "Marco, your grandmother is lovely. I can see many of her features in you."

Marco squeezed my hand. "Thank you for your kind comment. I adored her. Let's walk down this hall just a little further. There's someone else I'm anxious for you to meet."

We walked by a few more formal portraits of royal men, women, and soldiers before we stopped under the portrait of another royal lady much younger than his Nona. This lady was in her late teens or early twenties. I stared as Marco introduced us.

"Lana, I'd like you to meet your ancestor, Marchesa Genolli."

He caught me off guard to say the least. I never in my wildest dreams imagined Marchesa as a young woman. I took a few steps back and let go of his hand to get a better view of the painting. She had smooth fair skin, large green eyes, and the tiniest waist I have ever seen. I studied her features. I was curious only having heard stories about my ancestor and her pendant. I never knew what she looked like especially as a young vibrant woman in love. I did indeed inherit her red curly hair and green eyes. And what's this? She *is* wearing my pendant with an emerald- green gown and holding an adorable small dog. Curious for more details, I listened as Marco continued.

"She was the most beautiful lady of her time and the envy of every other royal lady in Venice. As I look at you, I see you have inherited many of her lovely facial features. You have her piercing green eyes, her stunning red curly hair, and her refined features like those of a true Venetian royal."

I studied the portrait again and asked. "I see she's holding a dog. Was that her dog or just a prop for the artist?"

Marco smiled. "I believe I told you from a very early age Marchesa loved animals, especially cats and dogs. The dog she is holding in her portrait is her precious 'Volpino Italiano' or also called 'Little Italian Fox' named 'Nicco.' For as long as Nicco was alive, Marchesa refused to go anywhere without him."

I stood back a little further to get a better view of Nicco. Nicco was as beautiful a dog as she was a lady. He was small with a fuzzy beige coat and resembled a small Spitz or perhaps a Pomeranian. I looked at Marco. "Odd, I've never heard of this breed before. He was very cute and by the smiles on his and Marchesa's faces, I can tell they loved each other very much. Tell me is this breed still present in Venice in my time?"

"Yes, it is. It almost became extinct but some determined animal lovers fought to prevent that from happening. We Italians, especially Venetians, are an incredibly determined lot so that's why we succeed at whatever we pursue. You know we have many dogs roaming our city pathways loose. Some of them have homes while others are strays. They don't have to worry about getting injured unless they fall into a canal because we have few buggies or carts or even streets for that matter. The same holds true in your time. Anyway, Marchese's Nicco is champagne colored, but the Volpino's fur can be white, black, or reddish. It's the perfect choice for a royal lady because they are small and grow to weigh no more than nine to twelve pounds.

"Venetians have always loved and respected our canine friends. That is why every year we honor Saint Roch who, in the fourteenth century, came to a town near Rome called Piacenza during the plague to heal the sick. When he fell ill himself, the town banished him. He had to seek refuge in a nearby forest where he could only access drinking water from a miraculous spring but had no food. The dog of a local nobleman was wandering in that forest and discovered Saint Roch. The canine brought him bread and licked his wounds until he got better. Among his many titles, Saint Roch is the patron saint of dogs, and his statue always has a dog standing next to him carrying a loaf of bread in its mouth. Italians commemorate and celebrate his life every autumn and invoke his spirit to protect us from the plague returning."

Always being fascinated with a piece of history I knew nothing about I asked, "Did any other famous Italians own a Volpino?"

Marco nodded. "Ah, my beautiful librarian and historian I love that you're always curious. The answer to that is 'yes.' Many who knew the artist Michelangelo claimed that a small dog resembling a Pomeranian but believed to be a Volpino liked to sit and watch Michelangelo paint. What a lucky dog he was!"

I laughed. "You can say that again. I would have loved to be a tiny flea on his head so I could watch as well."

Marco smiled. "Marchesa should be of special interest to you especially since she is wearing your pendant. The Doge of her time commissioned the painting as soon as she and my ancestor became betrothed. Two weeks after the completion of this portrait, their families called the engagement off.

"At the time of the young couple's break-up, anyone who knew about her pendant desired it. Rumors abounded that it held the key to a past Doge's treasure. One of her nephews, Enrico, tried to take the pendant while she slept in hopes of stealing the treasure for himself. Marchesa was a light sleeper and awoke only to beat him off with a broom she kept next to her bed for such emergencies. Some years later after another attempt on her life, one that almost proved successful, she decided to leave her beloved Venice and take her children from her marriage to a local businessman with her. In the middle of one night, they boarded a Venetian vessel sailing from Persia to Le Florida, a Spanish colony in the New World. Her husband, not wanting to lose track of them, followed his family on another ship to the same destination.

"Marchesa enjoyed her new life in The New World and died surrounded by her family at the age of sixty which at that time was considered a long life. She dictated the order of inheritance for her pendant just before she died."

I shook my head in awe. "I had no idea she fled in fear of being killed and how brave she was to do so. I never gave my personal history much thought, just thinking my necklace was a traditional family heirloom passed down through normal channels."

My eyes darted to the small portrait next to hers intrigued by why the subject was placed between the royals. "Why is that small portrait of a cat next to Marchesa's?"

Marco responded. "That's not just any cat; he was a royal

cat and Marchesa's other beloved pet. She named him 'Oro' which means gold in Italian. She chose that name because as a calico cat, Oro displayed large patches of orange fur which glowed in the sunlight like gold. She hoped to hold them both in her arms for her formal portrait, but being petite, the artist told her that he needed to concentrate on her, or so the story goes, so he offered to paint Oro a portrait of his own. That made Marchesa happy, and the artist was elated that he could finish her portrait. When finished, she requested that her beloved Oro's portrait hang next to hers in the palazzo's gallery. Mystics believe Oro really did have nine lives as the saying goes because he's been spotted in different times through the centuries."

"You're serious, aren't you? You're not going to believe me, but after one of the first times your shadow followed me, a Calico cat with those exact same markings crossed my path. Could it have been Oro's spirit?"

"When it comes to spirits, anything is possible especially since he belonged to your ancestor Marchesa. Maybe she was sending you a message not to be afraid of me through Oro." Marco took my hand. "Come there's more to see."

We walked a few steps further to a portrait of two young men in colorful military uniforms standing across from each other and holding swords upright in a salute. I studied the painting before asking, "Marco, who are those men? One of them looks like a much younger version of the man who called himself Reeno and came into the library to leave a message for you. At the time, he stated he knew you quite well. For some strange reason, I had a bad feeling about him so that was why I denied knowing you. Is he a Traveler as well?"

"He was the one who came to see you in the library? The same man in that portrait? Are you sure?" Marco's voice reflected his surprise and grew louder.

"Yes, I told you about him several times in the past week.

The last time I saw him was the day we Traveled. He didn't have a beard like in this painting, only a well-groomed mustache."

Marco watched as I ran my fingers over the painting's smooth, antique, embossed silver frame. He sighed. "I do remember you telling me about someone named Reeno. His proper name is Rinaldo. I never knew him by any other name. I can't wrap my head around why he followed me. We have known each other since childhood. His attitude changed for the worse right before I Travelled. My grandfather served his father The Doge as his Chief Council. This painting of Rinaldo and his younger brother Roberto was painted when his family resided in The Doge's palace. That was the happiest time of their lives. After his father's death, they, along with their mother, had to move out to accommodate the next Doge's family. Rinaldo's family was not rich by royal standards and had to move into a designated housing area for common working people. Rinaldo and his brother claimed they knew about the treasure and felt entitled to it since their father had given it to my grandfather. Both brothers warned me that if I find it, I had better hand it over as soon as I do, or they would make my life miserable perhaps even kill me.

"Rinaldo felt more determined about this than Roberto, so much so he continued his threats for quite a while after Roberto backed off. The younger brother believed those threats against me were wrong and stepped aside, leaving Rinaldo to carry them out alone. Roberto was always more respectful of the laws and of the church and entered the priesthood soon after this happened. Shocked by Rinaldo's actions, I felt relieved when later he took his threats back and apologized saying the remarks were made 'in the heat of the moment.'"

That last statement made me remember something Marco told me earlier. I hesitated but felt compelled to ask about one of his past statements since it still confused me. "You said you died not too long after finding the box. I don't understand.

How? You're so young. Did you fall ill? Was it from a shock? You're standing here with me now and appear to be in the best of health."

Marco squeezed my hand. "Two nights after The Doge's Carnival Ball, I went up to my room to check on the box. Just as I took it out of my hiding place, I heard heavy footsteps stomping up the back stairs and approach my door. The intruders were loud because they wanted to frighten me by letting me know they were coming. I had the forethought to place the treasure back in its hiding place right before two intruders broke down my bedroom door. My sword leaned against the corner of my desk where I kept it for personal safety. I reached for my sword at the precise moment those two masked intruders, dressed all in black and wearing face masks, surged in unannounced.

"The taller of the two spoke in a deep, muffled voice. 'If you hope to live a long and happy life, tell us where the treasure is. We're sure you know.' He then grabbed me from behind and held his sword across my throat. He pressed it against my throat so hard, I lost my breath and choked. Even with all his attempts to harm me, I refused to respond to his commands, so he continued his threats. 'Go get it and give it to me at once or we'll have to kill you.'

"He let me go but shoved me face down on the floor. Gasping for air, I tried to stand just as the shorter intruder who had remained silent this entire time pointed the tip of his sword at my heart. I knew they outnumbered me, but I continued to resist their ultimatums. I had promised to protect my grandfather's secret and remained resolved to do so. I shoved that sword aside and stood. They faced me, drew their swords, and each took turns plunging their weapons at me. They alternated positions, coming at me from all different directions, trying to confuse me. I was adept enough at fencing to avoid physical contact for a brief while. I leaped on my bed so I could keep watch on the changing directions of their individual attacks. They continued to dance on either side of me, so I jumped up and down on the bed trying to confuse them by alternating my sword's thrust between the two of them.

"Our swords clashed. First, I fought off the tall one on my right, then the shorter one on my left. I was able to wound the taller one by slicing a cut in his arm before piercing his leg. He fell to the ground screaming in pain. The smaller one gasped in what to me sounded like a high-pitched voice, like that of a young boy. He jumped up onto the section of the bed where I stood and proceeded to thrust his sword at me. He continued until his sword sliced my wrist at an artery, which started pouring out blood, thus making it more difficult for me to fight.

"I still refused to give up. This duel was important to me for my family's honor, our claim to the treasure, and my promise to my grandfather. I leaped forward and pointed my sword directly at him. He backed off for a moment before he jumped toward me again. He was short enough to reach my chest with his sword and stabbed me in the heart. I fell to the floor and died. They still would not be able to locate the treasure since I did not tell them anything before I died. I remained on the floor for a short time motionless and not breathing until surprised I felt the deep strain of my soul leaving my body. As I floated over my human form, I felt a strong, cold wind blowing in my direction, keeping my spirit hovering in that same air space. I didn't realize that Othero had sent that wind to keep my spirit in limbo as a shadow and return to him as such.

"As I already told you, Othero was relentless in his search for that key. Once he located the key, he sent my shadow to your psychic Aurellia."

Marco sighed before he continued. "I know that Othero chose the right wizard for me because as soon as my shadow arrived in Aurellia's presence, she pinpointed your exact location. She instructed me to shadow you for quite a while without calling attention to myself. Predicting the accident moments before it occurred, she diverted me to your accident scene at once. Obtaining your pendant was the reason I followed her directions, but I fell in love with you from the first moment I laid eyes on you. That was not supposed to happen. Aware no one else could see me but you, I moved you to safety and decided to stay and protect you from any further injury or even death rather than steal your pendant. The entire time I stayed with you I could hear Othero's voice whisper in my ear. 'This is your best chance Marcello, steal that pendant and keep that promise to your grandfather. Look at her, she's unconscious.'

"I never wanted any harm to come to you. As soon as I knew you were all right, I left without the pendant much to Othero's dismay. When Aurellia realized I couldn't steal your necklace, she at once put a spell on your friend Sara so she would seek the psychic's help to get through the nightmares caused by her divorce. Aurellia wanted Sara to recommend her to you and send both you and your pendant to her."

Stunned after listening to all of this, I gazed into his light brown eyes and squeezed his arm just to be sure this wasn't a dream. "Marco that's quite a story especially why Sara sent me to Aurellia, but you're here with me now. How could you be dead?"

"As long as I stayed with you after your accident, Aurellia allowed me to resume my true human form because we both sensed how frightened you might be of my shadow. That's why you saw me as an EMT and that's the reason we have Traveled back in time to four days before my death. If I only had that key before my duel, I might have been able to change my destiny and save my life.

"Your locket will help me unlock that box, finish my pledge to my grandfather, and protect my spirit's journey so I can remain here with you as a real person. I already mentioned that tomorrow evening Carnival season opens with the Ball at the Doges' Palace. I repeat that it would be the greatest honor of my life to be your escort."

My mind bounced back and forth attempting to assimilate all this latest information. I continued to remain in a state of denial about everything in my life and his. I had finally found the love of my life, and he was dead. I was so in love with him, I decided to accept his invitation. I wondered how much time we would still have left together. Every second became precious. Those thoughts made me no longer concerned about my shyness and lack of social skills but only of our love. I looked into his eyes. "Yes Marco, I would love to go to the Ball with you."

Marco leaned in and kissed my cheek. "You have made me the happiest man in Venice, in the world for that matter. I'll make sure you are the best dressed, most bejeweled woman there. Let me escort you back to your room. You'll be in for a long and wonderful day of pampering tomorrow."

We strolled back through the magnificent hall of paintings. Marco walked me down the open hallway and stopped by my bedroom door. He kissed my cheek before moving his lips to meet mine. Marco embraced me ever so tight before kissing me goodnight.

"Lana, having your pendant before the duel must work this time...for me...for us. I know you love me as much as I love you and I love you more than life itself."

I nodded before we kissed again. This time he deepened the kiss, "Until tomorrow, my love."

I opened my bedroom door and walked inside, exhausted from hearing all these new revelations and wondering if I had to choose between our love and my mother's legacy, my pendant. On the surface that might seem like an easy choice. Of course,

I'd choose Marco's love no matter what, but if he never returns, my mother's legacy is gone forever with him.

I worried we might have only two more days together as I undressed completely for bed. Before I could put on a night-gown, I heard a faint knock on my door. A voice whispered. "It's Marco."

I threw on the crimson silk robe draped over my bed post and went to the door. Opening it a crack, I looked into his dreamy eyes that stared back into mine. When it came to Marco, I had no willpower. Just the sight of him made my body ache with desire. Of course, I would let him in, we might only have a short time left together.

Marco closed the door and locked it. He picked me up in his strong arms and carried me to my bed. We lay down together before he unfastened the ties to my robe. I lay there naked, desiring him with my every breath. He kissed me. I closed my eyes as I felt the soft touch of his fingers slide down my entire body. My body tingled as if lightning raced through my veins. His kisses moved down my neck, until they lingered to kiss each breast. My body exploded with the fire of my deep passion for him.

His lips kissed every part of me before they traveled back up my neck to meet mine for a deep, lingering kiss. We caressed and held each other tight as he stared into my eyes with unrelenting passion. Standing, he undressed before we made love with feel-ings that had more meaning than ever before for the both of us realizing our time together might prove all too brief.

"I love you more than you can imagine," he whispered and kissed me one more time before he stood, dressed, and leaned down to whisper in my ear.

"I must leave now before anyone knows I was here. I don't want to stain your reputation with my household staff. My era is much stricter than yours about love and romance. Tomorrow, my love, I promise, will be the most exciting day and night of your life. The Ball will mesmerize you with its beauty and celebration. I will ask Sofia to spoil you, pamper you, and present you with the most beautiful clothes and jewelry. Remember we shall meet at seven at the wine bar not too far from the entrance to the ballroom. Your escort will know where that is. Until then..."

He took my hand and kissed it. I was breathless, speechless, funny how he did that to me. I watched him unlock the bedroom door and leave. I rolled over, placed my head on the overstuffed feather pillow, but had trouble falling asleep wondering who I had really fallen in love with and what the next two days would reveal.

CHAPTER
EIGHT

When I awoke the next morning Marco's words echoed in my mind. "Tomorrow, my love, I promise will be the most exciting day and night of your life." Just spending precious time with him made any day exciting. Once I cleared my head and focused, I pulled the chain connected to the bell near my night table. After a few minutes, Sofia knocked on my door. "I have your morning tea, my lady. May I come in?"

I tied the sash that fastened my robe before I went to the door and unlocked it. "Please do." I responded as I held the door open for her. She carried in a sterling silver tray with a pink and green China teapot and matching cup along with a small plate of homemade anise biscuits.

She shook her finger at me. "Lady Lana, you must be careful how many of Gracia's biscuits you eat this morning, or you will not fit into the beautiful gowns I have selected to show you in a short while."

I sat at my desk that doubled as a table and let Sofia serve me in style. I asked. "What is Count Banelli doing this morning?"

"He left for the palace very early this morning. All the arrangements for the ball are his responsibility. Our Doge relies on him because he is like an adopted son to him. Our current ruler is compassionate and cares about the family of his predecessor. Signore Rinaldo, the son of the former Doge, is likely there as well helping since he and our count have known each other since they were toddlers. A perfectionist, our Doge wants everything to be right for tonight's celebration. That's why he trusts our count to make that happen."

"That's quite an honor." I responded happy to hear about The Doge's opinion of Marco though still somewhat apprehensive about Rinaldo's role in the event. Since Sofia remained with me through breakfast, I didn't want her to detect any of my concerns about Marco's safety. My morning anise biscuits had a slight licorice flavor and were very tasty. I finished every crumb of my breakfast, wanted to lick my plate, before I gulped down the last spot of tea. Sofia advised me as she removed my tray.

"I'll return with some special ball gowns the count wishes you to view. He hopes you will first select the ones you would like to try on and ordered me to make you the star of the ball. Once we find the one that suits you best, I will make any necessary adjustments before I coordinate your jewelry and hair accessories. While I'm gone, please wash your face and comb your hair straight down. I'll return shortly to help you put on the appropriate undergarments."

I nodded and Sofia left me to my thoughts. *The star of the ball? Me?* I'm a mousey librarian from Naples, Florida. Hardly anyone I know would think of me in that way. Sofia must have a magic wand up her sleeve because she's going to need plenty of help.

She returned after a short while and knocked on my door. I opened it to see her carry in an armful of gowns all hung with the greatest care and in all shades of the rainbow and from my limited viewpoint in every style. Surprised by the amount and the beauty of them all, I blurted out. "They're all so lovely. How am I to choose?"

As Sofia passed by me, I held my hand out to feel all the luxurious fabrics. "Where did all these gowns come from?"

Sofia gave a quick curt reply before placing the gowns across my pillow. "You are not the only beautiful woman to be courted by our count. He has courted many in his lifetime prior to meeting you. Some were duchesses, some princesses, while others the daughters of the most powerful men in Venice. Each young lady hoped Count Banelli would choose her to be his countess. Almost every woman in Venice wants to marry him.

"My count prides himself on being caring and generous. As you can see by the number of gowns, he had many romantic trysts. He always told me he wanted the women in his life to look as beautiful as possible whether for formal events or to accompany him to important royal meetings and ordered me to make a special gown for each of them. Once worn, I ordered our laundress to clean each one before storing them for a future event. My count, always the perfect gentleman and having an excellent tailor such as myself in his employ, wanted gowns that would make the women he escorted stand out. Since the women were similar in dress size, I would make a few nips and tucks, and the dresses were ready to wear again by a different woman for a different occasion. I made all the gowns by hand, so that's why I appreciate your comments about their beauty.

"I have seen him with many women, but he could not find the right one to marry much to the disappointment of these women and their fathers. After he ended his romance with each of them, he told his closest staff members at that time that he lost interest in them because they did not meet his needs for a royal countess but most importantly for someone he could love. There are many special women that work right here in the palazzo, but none were lucky enough to catch his eye."

She cleared her throat. "I have never seen him look at a woman the way he looks at you. I hope you know how lucky you are." With that, she cast me a cold stare.

"*Almost every woman in Venice wants to marry him.*" Her comment made me wonder how that would bode for my chances.

Sofia continued. "Now you asked how will you choose the perfect dress? That will be the easy part. I will hold each one up in front of me. If you see one that pleases you, I'll place it in the middle of the bed for you to try on after we have viewed them all. The ones you don't like, I'll place over the chair near the window. My system of selection is quite simple but first we must deal with the undergarments."

I stood and she helped fasten all the stays to the most uncomfortable undergarments I have ever worn in my entire life. After my final ouch she said, "Sorry about the pain but we have to make your waist as small as possible."

Looks like she enjoyed that part of my dressing, especially the part about me not breathing. I glanced back at all the formal dresses. They reminded me of the most elegant costumes in a romantic period movie with all their ruffles, frills, and gorgeous material. I must have appeared lost in a daydream because Sofia had to touch my arm to get my attention so she could start the fashion show. The first gown she held up was a mauve silk fitted gown with deep purple and pink beading across the neckline and ruffles along the hemline. I liked that one so on the bed it went. She then showed me a bright yellow taffeta one with a full skirt. It did not take long for me to reject it. "It's lovely but not with my red hair," I added. She placed that one on the chair. A very stylish black taffeta was next. "Sofia, that one is so very elegant but black is too dismal for such a happy event." She nodded in agreement. A royal blue crepe with a high neckline, one that would look beautiful with my locket, was next. I loved it, so we put that one the bed as well as a white crepe gown with a design of peach flowers down the right side. When we finished, I had four to try on and seven to put back.

Sofia touched her forehead. "Oh, my lady, how could I

forget? Count Banelli selected a very distinctive one for you. Wait just a few minutes longer to make up your mind."

She dashed out into the hall and came back in right away carrying a long, beige linen bag. When she removed the bag, I saw the most beautiful emerald- green satin gown with a ruffled neckline and train. Odd I thought that dress looked familiar. Oh my gosh! I had to place my hands over my mouth not to gasp at my complete surprise. That dress was the same emerald-green dress the woman with red hair wore in the illustration of the Carnival Ball and that was the same dress I wore in my dream. But how could that be?

We tried on my other selections first. They were all so lovely I couldn't choose between them. Sofia encouraged me to try on the emerald- green gown. "Please my lady, try on my count's choice for you. It may help you make up your mind. When he selected this dress, he remarked how green enhances your beautiful eyes and complements your fair complexion."

Could he have known it was the same dress as in the illustration I showed him in the library? With so many unusual occurrences flying all around me, it was possible. I tried it on, and we both agreed the emerald- green gown flattered me the most. Sofia looked at me. "Take a look in the tall mirror. Turn around so you can see the beautiful ruffles along the back. My count has an excellent eye for beauty in clothing and everything in his life."

As I turned to take another look, the memory of that illustration popped into my mind. I tried to rationalize the decision for my selection. I refused to believe that either the illustration, or my dream was the reason, but that Marco thought the emerald- green gown flattered me the most. His choice worked for me. Who else did I aim to please?

Once I selected my gown for this evening's ball, Sofia treated me to a full day of pampering and primping. As the time for my appearance at the ball grew closer, Sofia dismissed the young women who washed my hair and helped me bathe. I smelled as fragrant as the lily petals they used for my bath.

Sofia gave my hair a quick towel dry before she brushed it out. Once my pampering was complete, she helped me get back into those uncomfortable undergarments by fastening all the stays in the bodice before I put on that beautiful gown and a pair of gold, sparkly evening shoes. Sofia asked, "Please sit on the stool near the dressing table and face me so I could apply your rouge, lip rouge, and finish styling you hair." Make-up complete, she styled my long hair up with combs and curled the ends before adding emerald- green silk rosettes to both sides. She removed a small black velvet pouch from her skirt pocket. "I made you something special for tonight. I found the left-over pieces of material I kept after I made this gown and sewed a ruffled choker adding the same color sequins to match your gown."

Sophia opened the pouch and held up a beautiful choker in that same emerald- green material. She handed it to me for my approval. "I love it. How sweet that you thought of me. I'd love to wear it. It's exquisite. The dim candlelight of this room makes the sequins sparkle like fireworks."

Sophia advised. "I'll be delighted to put it on you but first you much take off your pendant. Don't worry. I'll keep it safe for you in this velvet pouch. You can trust me. The count trusts me with all his jewelry. The choker will show much better wearing only one necklace."

Take off my necklace? I have never taken it off since the day my mother gave it to me. Aurellia's warning came to mind. "Let the stone's powers take charge in your life so they can go to work for you but remember never to take your locket off. Always wear it even to bed. There may be others with bad intentions who also seek what secrets Marchesa's locket holds."

I handed Sofia the choker. "I'd love to wear the choker, but I will keep my locket on as well. I never take it off as you noticed, not even for a bath. I wear it in memory of my mother."

An odd expression crossed Sofia's face. "Very well my lady, as you wish. I only wanted you to look your best. Please stand and face the mirror so I can fasten the choker."

I did as she asked. When I looked into the mirror, I remained amazed at how beautiful I looked even without the choker. Once again, she had transformed me from a mousy librarian into a princess. Sofia then fastened the choker around my neck. I beamed because I felt like Cinderella. My smile must have said it all because Sofia nodded. "I'm glad you approve of my work. I appreciate your confidence in my service."

She then went into the closet and took out an ornate Carnival mask of a fairy queen, its face painted in peach, powder blue, and emerald- green positioned on a wooden stick. "I almost forgot. This is your most important accessory for tonight's party. You will need to hold this mask up to your face all night. When you arrive at the Ball, cover your face with it. Since that has been our custom, many unexpected romances blossomed between two masked strangers."

As she handed me the mask, she informed me. "It's now half past six. When you tell me, I'll inform your guard that you are ready for his escort."

Holding up my beautiful Carnival mask to my face, I took another quick peek in the mirror still wondering what my evening had in store for me. I wanted Sofia to know how grateful I was. "Thank you again, Sofia, I appreciate all you did for me especially since I'm not a royal and had no idea what to expect this evening. I'll never forget this. Since I'm as ready as I'll ever be, please call for my escort."

Sofia nodded, curtsied, and left. Not too long after she did, I heard a knock on my chamber door. Marco had already informed me that he had pre-arranged for one of his personal guardsmen to escort me to our meeting point in the ballroom.

When I opened my chamber door, a most handsome young man in uniform greeted me. "Good evening my lady. My name is Enzo, and I am Count Banelli's personal guard. He requested I escort you to a specific meeting point in the ballroom." He held out his arm. "May I?"

When I held onto Enzo's arm, I felt like a queen as he escorted me out of the palazzo to the exterior stairway that led to the dock. "Careful my lady, the step down into the gondola is not as easy as it appears," he advised after getting into the gondola first. Then, he reached for both my arms to help me step into a beautiful shiny black and gold gondola decorated with multi-colored streamers and fresh chrysanthemums in lavender and white. Their sweet smell permeated the air as our gondola floated down the canal that led to the Doge's Palace. All along the way, I took in the ambiance of the evening, looking at all the colored lanterns on the docks, the people walking by in elegant costumes and capes, and all the many stars in the clear night sky. Enzo pointed to my mask as a reminder. He kept his bright, metallic silver one attached to his face, tied by black ribbons on each side of his mask to the back of his head. "Remember it is the tradition of Carnival that no-one should guess your true identity." I quickly held my mask up to my face as more people walked by us.

When we reached the Palace, two of the Doge's attendants came to greet us and pulled the gondola by its ropes close to the dock. Enzo helped me step out of the gondola and walked with me down the long dock to the equally lengthy stairway which led into the palace.

I looked up at that impressive building. It was even more breathtaking all lit up at night. The illustrations in that large volume didn't do it justice. I almost tripped because I couldn't stop looking up, trying to absorb all its beauty and opulence.

As we entered the magnificent ballroom, two different masked guards greeted us. I stared at all the fresh red and white roses in the Venetian glass wall sconces and in vases on the marble tables. Soft candlelight gave the cream walls an ivory glow. As I looked up, I held my breath marveling at the magnificent ceiling of mirrored smoked glass with gold gilded patterns all along it. The walls held large canal scenes of Venice by Italian Masters. Being inside The Doge's Palace made me feel like I was walking into a beautiful dream. I glanced forward overcome by the beauty yet to come.

Deep rose brocade drapes hung from the ceiling's tall glass doors, their color enhanced by the contrasting white marble dining tables. Gilded high back chairs graced each table. Smaller marble tables to set wine glasses on encircled the wooden dance floor. As Enzo and I approached my meeting point, we heard the soulful sounds of musicians playing mandolins while a tenor sang Venetian love songs. I searched for my handsome count, catching the eyes of every man I passed. Finally, I saw Marco standing by an arched doorway next to the wine bar, our meeting point. I held my mask closer to my face, but I was sure he would recognize me from my dress and hair.

Marco looked regal wearing an exquisite white, royal blue, and gold mask of a warrior which from where I stood only enhanced his presence. As soon as he spotted us, he walked over to greet us. Nodding to Enzo, he said. "Thank you, my trusted guard, for escorting this lovely lady to me." With that, Enzo bowed and left. Marco then took my hand and led me to one of the small tables before he signaled for a server. "Please bring us two glasses of sparkling wine."

The server returned with two red crystal flutes filled with sparkling white wine. As Marco handed me one of the beautiful glasses, I peeked through the eye holes of his mask and could see how his eyes sparkled at my transformation. He took my hand. "My love, you are a feast for my eyes. You look beautiful. I shall be the envy of every man at the ball."

I blushed so deeply that heat rushed to my cheeks. It wasn't difficult for me to return his complement. "Marco, you're so handsome in your military uniform. I know I *am* the envy of every woman here." After I spoke, I lowered my gaze into my matching silk fan as I imagined a proper Venetian lady would do.

"Lana, let's share a toast to our romantic evening," he said softly. I nodded as he toasted our wonderful evening ahead. "May tonight's ball be the beginning of our wonderful and long-lasting love."

He took my glass from my hand, escorted me to a secluded table, and positioned my train to help me sit. Marco gazed at me with pure love in his eyes. "Please Lana, I'd like for you to enjoy another taste of this most incredible drink."

He handed me my crystal flute. At first, I sipped slowly as I did after our toast. I had never sampled sparkling wine before since that was a luxury neither my parents nor any of my few dates could afford. It seemed the more I sipped, the sweeter and more delicious the wine tasted, until I finished the entire glass all at once.

"Oh my! Marco, please help me I feel lightheaded." I tried to stand but Marco caught me when I almost collapsed and whisked me back onto my feet. He smiled as he joked. "It can be dangerous to drink so fast but by doing so, I take it you liked our wine."

I waved one arm in the air as he held me. "I loved it." I mumbled. Marco laughed. "I think you're a little tipsy. Come my sweet, let's join the other couples and dance before your head begins to spin some more."

Tipsy or not, how could I refuse his invitation? My vision was just a bit blurry but from where I stood Marco looked even more dashing in his formal, royal blue fitted jacket with gold buttons and matching trousers. He also wore a matching royal blue velvet cape which opened in the front and draped to the floor. With his help, I steadied myself and slowly followed him onto the dance floor. We danced a waltz holding up our masks and following the other elegant couples dressed in all the colors of the rainbow around the ballroom dance floor. My vision cleared after our dance just in time to see Rinaldo, his supposed friend, approach dressed in black silk with a black and white mask that had the unsettling image of a protruding bird's beak. Marco recognized him even with the obnoxious mask. His partner, a woman dressed in the same sapphire blue gown with a ruffled neckline that her counterpoint wore in that book's illustration, remained silent.

How can this be? They looked like they had just stepped out of that page about the Ball. Too much wine or have I lost my mind? The more I looked at her, the faster my heart pounded. Peculiar, I felt as if I knew her even though she never took off the beautiful gold mask of an Egyptian princess which covered her face. Marco greeted Rinaldo with a quick nod before introducing him to me. I turned my back to them both briefly to get a tighter grip on my mask hoping Rinaldo wouldn't recognize me, but Marco spoiled my attempt at anonymity.

"Rinaldo, please meet Lana, the most wonderful and beautiful woman I have ever met. Please, my love, turn around and lower your mask."

I did as Marco requested, not wanting to appear out of place. Just as I had feared, Rinaldo registered instant recognition. His eyes dropped like rain from my face to my pendant as he took my hand, raised it to his lips, and kissed it. That made me uncomfortable to say the least especially when he said. "Lana, you have such a kind way about you, I feel like we have met before."

I lowered my eyes. "Thank you for the compliment. We may have in another lifetime."

Rinaldo turned and asked his date to come forward and meet us. She still refused to take off her mask, which seemed odd to me, but her voice sounded as familiar as Rinaldo's.

"Marco, Lana, please meet Anna, my dance partner for this wonderful celebration."

Anna curtsied and whispered in a low voice. "Charmed to meet you both."

The couple chatted with us for a short while. After they left to get drinks, I asked Marco. "Does he introduce all his dates as dance partners?"

Marco laughed. "Rinaldo has so many women lined up to date him, they would wrap all the way around this palace. Come, enough about him. Let's enjoy our evening and dance."

He took my hand and led me onto the dance floor. We danced slowly to the soulful love songs of the musicians. A dream could not have been so sweet. We circled the dance floor in line with all the other dancers. The women wearing gowns in every primary color held onto their trains as they swayed to the beat of those slow love songs. After a few more dances, the musicians took a short break. Rinaldo and his dance partner made their way through the other couples to us again. She still wore her mask tied behind her head with black ribbons.

Rinaldo had removed his. *Just like their counterparts in the book...was my mind playing tricks on me?* I didn't have time to rationalize anything because as we stood and chatted, the other dancers assembled around us.

The musicians resumed playing and the dancers formed a semicircle around us. *I must be dreaming. They assembled exactly as they had in the print.* They clapped their hands and chanted "Marco...Marco." He bowed and grabbed onto my arm. I had no idea what kind of dance we were going to do, especially since the tempo picked up. I was so clumsy I worried about falling wearing these gold evening shoes but was able to follow Marco without too much distress. We danced and everyone clapped to the music before they joined us.

We swirled around the dance floor, happy to be in each other's arms until we could hardly stand. Marco looked into my eyes as our last slow dance ended, and the musicians announced they were about to take another break. He whispered in my ear. "Come, my love, let's take a walk. I'd like to show you how beautiful my city is at night."

We left the dance floor and walked out through the two huge doors that led to a circular balcony. At once, I recognized it from the many illustrations in history books as the royal balcony where the Doge and his wife waved to the gondolas below. When I gazed up, stars filled the night sky. It was such a clear evening; it seemed like every star in the universe twinkled. I pointed to two shooting stars. "Look at those beautiful shooting stars. I've heard they bring good fortune and their trail of light points here to our love."

Marco hugged me. "You know my Nona always said shooting stars were a good omen."

He placed my arm in his and walked me to the stone wall near the edge of the canal. We stopped and he pulled me closer. "I love you, Lana. We've shared so much in such a brief time together. By now you must know how deep my feelings are for you, not just because of your beauty, but for your calmness, grace, and the strength you demonstrated in your personal tragedy. As I already told you, Aurellia did send me to your accident scene but unfortunately, I was only able to protect you from dying. I wish I could have helped your loved ones. Your strength in enduring such a hardship remains an inspiration to me. Even in my shadow form, I wanted to reveal the truth about myself and tell you how much I love you."

Marco moved closer to me. A boyish smile crossed his face. "My most beautiful lady, I would like very much to kiss you right here under all of these flickering stars."

I nodded and closed my eyes, eager for our lips to meet. When they did, sparks flew across my heart and mind like those shooting stars we had just witnessed in the night sky. Marco had seized my heart with every ounce of my love in it. I became drunk with my desire for him. He sensed my feelings because he said. "Come with me to a secret place where we can spend time together alone."

He grabbed my hand and rushed us through the crowded ballroom. Our escape was beautiful, but, in an odd way, scary. It was beautiful because of the setting, but unsettling because in our rush, we bumped into some patrons whose costumes in dark colors and masks with exaggerated features frightened me.

We wove our way through the crowd until we reached the far end of the ballroom where we exited through a pair of magnificent doors with carvings of leaves and flowers high-lighted in gold on them that led into a long formal hallway. Portraits of past Doges lined the walls along our path. We walked by four of them before we stopped in front of a full-length mirror with a gold frame of carved flowers. When I gazed ahead, I saw more formal portraits and wondered why he chose to stop here.

Marco removed that beautiful mirror from the wall and placed it on the floor. I was surprised at how such a large mirror could be so light. He then pushed on the wall where the mirror hung. To my complete surprise, the wall swiveled around and opened to reveal a secret passageway. Marco winked and whis-pered, "Don't be afraid. I know my way around all these secret passageways quite well. Rinaldo and I spent many days here playing war games as boys."

Once we were inside that secret passageway, Marco turned, slid the mirror back across the opening, and posi-tioned it to hide the door before he closed and locked it behind us. I stood by speechless. I followed Marco's lead, and we walked down the colorful tiled hallway. I was wobbling a bit, and he had to grab onto me a few times to keep me from falling since I had on my thin-heeled formal shoes. We soon found ourselves going through a heavy wooden door with massive iron locks on one side that, when opened, revealed a very narrow, dark, bleak corridor with an uneven fieldstone floor.

"Lana, now we have entered the southern part of the palace. There is a more direct entrance to reach this point, but Rinaldo and I always liked the mystery of this entrance. We are about to enter the section of the palace known as The Pozzi or The Wells built hundreds of years ago to house prisoners. The further we walk down this corridor, the bleaker our atmosphere and surroundings will become and appear much gloomier than the beautiful ballroom we just left because we are in The Doge's prison. You will see firsthand what I mean."

"Marco, I don't understand why we're even here. Where are we going? This area is so dark and desolate, it frightens me. Why would you take me here on such an enchanted night of magic and romance?"

"Trust me, Lana. I would never let any harm happen to you. Where we are going is quite different from all of this. I want us to be alone in comfort to share our love where no one will find us."

His response was vague, again making me more concerned. As we entered this section of the palace, chills ran up my back. It was cold, damp, primitive, and very dark. The door that led to this section was composed of heavy wood with strong iron locks on the outside. As we proceeded further, Marco told me. "Lana, each one of these sturdy wooden doors on either side of us opens to one prison cell in the palazzo's prison. This row of cells is no longer in use. Some have hard wooden beds that can accommodate six prisoners at a time. Of course, there were no amenities and none of the luxuries we just left. As you can see, all the cells have windows protected by heavy crisscrossed iron bars that face this hallway."

I looked straight down this hallway. Just by the sheer number of doors, I knew there were too many prison cells in this section of the palazzo to count. I shivered from fear of how far down we were going. Marco stopped short in front of the very next door. He turned to me smiled and kissed my cheek. "Don't be afraid, my love. This special cell was reserved for royalty who needed privacy because they may have been awaiting trial, fell ill, or needed protection from an enemy. It is still in use that way. The cells on either side of it are left vacant for security."

He then took a large key from his cape pocket, placed it in the lock, and jiggled the door open. He grabbed my waist and whisked me inside. I exclaimed surprised when I turned to get a better look. "Marco, this room is breathtaking!" I took in all its beauty. "This room could easily be inside the palazzo with its pale rose wallpaper, colorful Persian rug, and that amazing four-poster double bed with a canopy."

The more I looked the more I couldn't believe all the luxurious amenities. The bed had fancy rose colored linens, multiple pastel pillows, and a thick mattress. There was even a step stool. I gasped. "I can't imagine why something this beautiful would be in the center of such bleak surroundings. How did you find this?"

He looked at me, "As I already told you, growing up, Rinaldo and I played war games in those other empty prison cells. We knew this entire section well and knew this room was reserved for royal use and where its spare key was kept. One time, we had to make a run for it because a duke was coming to recuperate from a bad cough. This room is always beautiful, always kept immaculate because the staff never knew when a royal would need to use it. Now please give me your hand."

I was so surprised by it all, I gasped. "This room could be a scene right out of a love story." Amazed by its ambiance, I continued to look at the paintings, the pottery, the royal tea service on the nightstand, but before I could say another word, Marco grabbed my hand and walked me further inside. He took off his long velvet cape, placed it over the soft bed, and dropped his mask. He turned to me, held his arms out, as his eyes pleaded with mine. "Lana, we can be alone here hidden from the partygoers and away from the noise. I want to show you how deep my love is for you. Here, we have all the time in the world. No one would ever think of looking for us here."

I sighed as I dropped my mask and fell into his open arms. He swept me up and kissed my lips before he helped me undress as he did the same. His kisses continued down my neck as he lifted me onto the bed. From that point on, we didn't have to say a word. Our feelings spoke for each of us. We lay naked on his soft cape and made love accompanied by the faint throbbing sounds of the ballroom musicians before falling asleep and staying there until the music stopped. When we awoke, Marco looked into my eyes.

"Lana, we love each other. With Othero's help, I know I can change my fate so we can be together for the rest of our lives. You must believe that's possible. If there's any way I can alter my shadow fate and become whole and alive again I will. For you...for us... I promise. I want to marry you and stay with you for the rest of my life."

He left me speechless. How could I have fallen in love with a shadow? I must have lost my mind because after fumbling for the right words, I said "Yes, Marco, I will marry you. I don't know how we'll make this work, but I always believed that true love could make anything happen."

Marco smiled and kissed me. "You have made me the happiest man in the world. We shall make wedding plans soon, but for now we must leave the palace before anyone finds us here."

Before anyone finds us here. My mind repeated those words, making our tryst even more dangerous and exciting. We dressed. Marco put on his cape before he pushed open that heavy door to our special room. After he locked it, we left through that dark hallway as quietly as we came, leaving behind no traces of our visit. When we reached the ballroom, we strolled through that magnificent room like we belonged there hoping no one would notice us. The colorful festoons and lovely flowers from last night's party covered the dance floor. Since the palace staff had their hands full, they paid no attention to us. Marco led me across the room to the front entrance that led to the docks. We walked to the Grand Canal where he signaled for one of the remaining gondolas reserved for guests to come for us. After helping me onboard, we rode back to his palazzo under the rays of the morning sun. We tiptoed inside not to wake the servants, and Marco escorted me to my bedroom door.

He told me before he left. "After you rest, I will need to discuss something of the utmost importance with you. We'll meet in four hours in the main sitting room by the fireplace. Is that all right with you?"

I nodded "yes" but noticed his eyes focused once again on my pendant. I was sure that was what our conversation would be about, but realized it was necessary if he wished to become whole again. My heart hoped he really did love me for me and not for that key. I guessed I would find out soon enough.

CHAPTER
NINE

Later that same morning, after what seemed an all too brief nap, I freshened up and met Marco in the main sitting room. Thinking he would ask for my pendant the precise moment he saw me, I remained cautious, but once again, he surprised me. Taking my hand, he reassured me. "Lana, this morning you are in for a wonderful treat. We're going to visit the real Venice, the one the visitors never see."

We walked out the front door of his palazzo to the main street that bordered the Grand Canal. He led me along that busy waterway before we turned to go on a narrow side street that took us to a small hill. Once at the bottom of the hill, we zig zagged across tiny walkways until we reached another very constricted side street. He walked so fast I could barely keep up with him through all our twists and turns. "Marco, please slow down. Where are we going?" I asked. "We've made so many quick turns, I'm getting dizzy."

He didn't answer but continued to walk at a brisk pace until we reached the end of the last narrow street. When I looked forward, I saw the most colorful and magnificent marketplace selling all kinds of things, spices, produce, flowers, handmade jewelry, clothes, even fresh seafood. The colorful vendor tables displayed an amazing and eclectic assortment of goods from all over the world. They were a collage of bright colors and textures for my eyes. I turned around to catch a glimpse of The Grand Canal not too far back in the distance, but I still had no idea where we were.

We took our time and sauntered through the different stands with fresh vegetables, spices, and crafts. Vendors called out to us hoping to get our attention. The myriads of smells, hues, and sounds from that busy marketplace seduced my senses. I wanted to stay longer and shop, after all I still am female no matter the century, but Marco hurried me past it all to a quiet area in a small park just a short distance away from all the hustle and bustle.

He led us to a bench where we sat. From there, I looked at that amazing town square, the marketplace, and the small garden of red and yellow flowers that surrounded us. We remained silent for a few moments but I'm sure we were both thinking about the same thing, my pendant, the key he needed to find the treasure and become whole again. Marco broke the silence first. He removed a small hourglass from his pants pocket and placed it on the bench between us. I became mesmerized watching those tiny grains of sand fall from the top glass to the bottom.

He looked into my eyes. "This hourglass represents our lives, our love, and will tell us how much time we now have left together. That time rests in your hands. Remember I told you I needed us to come back to Venice four days before those thieves try to kill me again. Othero advised me that knowing what to expect and how to respond would be the only way I could relive those days to my advantage. This will be my time to make things right, keep my promise to my grandfather, and return to you as a real man but that would only last so long as the sands in this hourglass. Everything rests on you giving me your pendant, the key, to open that box. Please Lana, think about it. Think about how happy we'll be and what a wonderful future is in store for us."

I looked down at the grass, confused by why I would even be torn between my ancestor's pendant which served as the key, and, more importantly, Marco's future which I hoped to share with him. I grasped my pendant and chain with both hands and looked deep into his eyes. "Marco, I will give you my necklace with all its powers and protective aura even though Aurellia advised me never to take it off because by doing so, those powers will no longer protect me. I want them to protect you because I love you with all my heart and want to keep you safe. Please understand my hesitancy. Change has always been diffi-cult for me because of all my past misfortunes. I just need a few minutes to compose myself and take it off."

As I tried to take off the key, my hands froze in place. It was just like in the library, when a new delivery came, my legs would freeze, not wanting to get up and face how much work was ahead, but this grip felt much tighter. I couldn't get my frozen hands to release my pendant. Frozen perhaps because I feared he wouldn't return, and I had already lost everyone else in my life that I loved.

He put his arm around me, and I rested my head on his shoulder. I whispered, "Hold my frozen hands in yours to help warm them so I can unlock my pendant and give it to you." He kissed the top of my head and whispered. "Be calm, close your eyes, my darling, and take a deep breath. Think about all the beauty we have just seen, the canal, the marketplace, and the flowers. Think about last night and how strong our love is for each other and how it will now remain so forever."

Since I trusted him, I closed my eyes. As he gently kissed my eyelids and warmed my hands, my world became so quiet so peaceful so wonderful...until suddenly...I felt the park bench moving. Was it a tremor? I opened them at once to see. We remained seated on that park bench but once again spun through the same darkness as the one through which we had arrived. When light brightened our journey, I saw we Traveled forward through time and just like before, people from different centuries marked our trip. Marco slid across the bench, reached over, and grabbed me as tight as he could. His arms tightened around my waist holding me back to prevent me from falling into the darkness. Round and round we spun. When it appeared like we were about to make a crash landing, my mind couldn't take any more. I became dizzy and passed out.

I woke up startled. Still unaware of where I was, I stretched my arms out straight and knocked over a large pile of books in the process. Surprised by all the noise that surrounded me, I lifted my head and looked around to find myself back at my desk in the library. I pinched my arm to make sure I wasn't dreaming. No, this was not a dream. I looked at my clothes! They were the same ones I had on the day I left, and my pendant and chain were still around my neck. An odd feeling came over me. *Did I really leave or was this all just a dream?* Everything in my world appeared the same as it did on that day. The patrons even spoke to me as if nothing unusual had happened.

I glanced down at the large book my head rested on. It was that same volume of Venetian history opened to the exact page which had formed that dark hole into which we fell. I sat back stunned. I shook my head trying to shake off the Travel dust while still hoping this entire episode was a dream. If it was, it was one darn good one. I looked down at the book again. That illustration of the couple who resembled us at The Doge's Ball replaced the dark hole. I heard someone approach. I quick looked over to see Marco pop out from behind one of the book-shelves carrying a book on antique Venetian jewelry. He brought it to my desk for me to check out. Before he handed it to me, he asked. "Are you all right? Did you have any problems from our Travel?"

I nodded. "I don't think so. I'm surprised but okay. You continue to amaze me. This was quite unexpected. I don't understand, why did we have to come back?"

Marco touched the top of my hand. "I'm sorry if I surprised you but I promise to explain everything. Please check this book out to me. It's only ten minutes until closing. I'll wait for you outside on the steps like I always do." I nodded and checked the book out to myself while another librarian closed the library.

I hurried to meet Marco outside. My thoughts spinning as I awaited his explanation; all the while, I tried to appear as normal and calm as possible. He placed the library book under one arm and put my arm under his other. "Please, come. Let's take a short walk."

Marco led us to our favorite spot in the park where we had our first date. Confused, I still wondered if everything that happened between us so far was real. We sat on that same bench...our bench...as Marco opened the history book and turned the page so I could see it.

"Please take a look at this illustration."

I moved closer to him on the bench as he explained. "This is an exact drawing of your pendant, the key, is it not? The text states no one since the time of Marchesa Genolli has seen that pendant. I'm sure it's because no one knew how to locate her, her heirs, or her necklace. She made her uncle, a shipping magnate, keep her passage to the New World a secret from both her contemporaries and her enemies. Othero had to work his most accomplished wizardry to pinpoint her precise destination in The New World. She came here to Le Florida to start a new life and travelled across the state to Naples. Her family grew up there, and she died there. So as stated in her will, the eldest daughter in each future generation would inherit the pendant and by doing so, would not make public knowledge its importance or location. That is why it came to you without any interference. You were the first to discuss anything about it with

Aurellia. A secret kept for hundreds of years, until you divulged it. That alone is amazing. Look at this. This is the formal portrait of Marchesa wearing your pendant that hangs in my palazzo."

Could it be true that no one has seen the key or even heard about it since Marchesa left Venice? I suppose so because as my mother told me that the women including herself who inherited the pendant kept it well hidden under their bodice on a long chain or refused to wear it at all because of fear of having it stolen. Unlike them, I wore mine openly to show how proud I am of my heritage. I guess that's how Marco found me. I glanced at the detailed drawing again. Indeed, that was my pendant. It was such a perfect match. A sudden uneasiness came over me. Marco took my hand and placed it in his.

"Lana, I'm now asking you again to make one of the toughest decisions of your life. Your pendant is your inheritance, your gift from your mother, and a link to your past. As you said, by giving it to me, its powers and auras will protect me so I can retrieve the crown, the valuable treasure that will solidify our happy future together. Once my promise to my grandfather is kept, I will become human again. I promise I *will* return to give the pendant back to you. That key can prevent my death so I will no longer have to live as a shadow, and we can then be together for the rest of our lives."

Tears streamed down my face as I held tightly onto my pendant, afraid to let my mother's legacy go, but I knew if I wanted a future with the love of my life, I had to trust him and give it to him.

"But Marco, I'm worried. How will I know if you succeed? I've already lost everyone in my life that I loved. I can't bear the thought of living without you, too. Please don't leave me. How will I know you won't be murdered again? You may not come back at all because you've returned to your shadow form again or 'moved on' as Aurellia explained to become a ghost? My mother's pendant is my link to my past and my family's future. I don't want to lose it, but I don't want to lose you, especially since I love you more than life itself."

Marco's eyes pleaded with mine. "You will lose me for sure and forever if I don't have that key. Without those powers, they'll kill me again. Only this time my fate will be locked into eternity and will never have another chance to return to human life."

He got down on his knees and removed a small, blue velvet box from his pocket.

"I've been saving this to give you after my return. You must trust me, Lana. I love you with all my heart. I'm no good to either of us as a shadow. My current human state will not last too much longer before they attempt to kill me again. Once I return with your pendant, I hope you will come back with me to my time in Venice, marry me, and be my countess, my partner, my wife."

Marco opened the small velvet box to reveal a platinum ring fit for a queen with a large oval diamond at its center surrounded by small blue sapphires.

"This was my grandmother's ring. She gave it to me before she died and told me. 'Once you find the love of your life, give my ring to her to signify your everlasting love.' Lana, you are that woman. I want to give you this ring, a precious part of my own family legacy. Will you marry me?"

He took that beautiful antique ring out of the box. I held out my left hand. Marco placed it on my ring finger, closed my hand, and kissed it. I was speechless as I still grasped my pendant with both hands.

I wanted to take my locket off and give it to him, but my fingers froze around it again and, just like before, I couldn't free them. I knew I could lose my mother's legacy but if I was lucky, I'd gain a future with the love of my life. I realized my mother's legacy was secure and life with a handsome shadow from the past very shaky, but I loved him and was willing to take that chance.

"Marco please help me unfasten my locket. My hands will not move." I sat back as my head spun like a child's top. I wondered why Marco did not rush to take it. He didn't pressure me. Instead, he held me close and hugged me.

As he did, I closed my eyes. His hug gave me peace as my mind drifted into a trance. My eyes remained closed, but my mind could still hear Marco's voice.

"Believe me, Lana. I can't have you return with me during this dangerous time. My situation is far too risky for you since I still have that target on my back. More than anything, I want to keep you safe.

"I must go back to my palazzo several hours before my murder to have enough time to make sure the treasure is secure and prepare to meet my killers. Because this day is in my future, Othero will wipe clean the memory of my murder from my servants' minds. The day will begin anew for them as it will for me. Since I know what to expect, I have the upper hand this time. Once my struggle is over and I defeat my enemies, I will return to you. But before that happens, I will send you a sign of my love."

As he spoke, his voice became softer and softer. His words became so far away, they were as quiet as a whisper. I remained in my dreamlike state for a few more minutes and listened to his every word until I no longer felt the warmth of his arms around me. I opened my eyes surprised by what I saw. *His melodic tones had swayed me into the most peaceful trance, and I didn't see him leave.*

Still amazed, I looked down at my blouse. My gold chain still hung around my neck, but my pendant was missing. He had freed my hands and took it while I slept. I became concerned, worried that I could lose him forever and began to sob so hard and for so long my eyes ached and burned from my tears. I pounded my fist repeatedly on the back of that park bench wanting to vent my frustration. I desperately wanted assurance that he would come back to me. How could I be so naïve? Marco was the first man I had given my heart to since college. Not only could I lose the love of my life but also my only link to my past. I sat there alone crying until darkness covered the sky. I refused to go straight home because I wanted to avoid thinking about all the happy memories we shared, unsure if they would happen again.

Once I calmed down, my mind convinced me not to get my hopes up because more than likely, I would never see him again or for that matter, my pendant. I decided to take the long way home. Devastated, I was in no hurry to get there. I remembered Marco told me that masked intruders who thought he possessed the key, murdered him to steal it and take the crown. Now that he had the key for real, he could die again, this time forever, and I would lose him forever. I cried. Pendant or no pendant, deception or not, I loved Marco with every breath I took and hoped he would come back to me.

I dragged myself home shuffling my feet the last few blocks from sheer exhaustion. My head down, my eyes flooded with tears once more. Since I now knew the truth about him, I wanted to see that shadow jump out from the bushes one more time and for us to start our relationship from the beginning but knew how impossible that was. Marco's safety consumed my mind and my heart.

I was one house away from my apartment when surprised by what I saw blurted out "Who's there?" A tall figure dressed in a hooded black raincoat ran from the front of my building down the street in the opposite direction from where I approached. I yelled "Stop! Why are you here? Don't go near that building! Go away!"

I couldn't tell if the hooded stranger was male or female but saw that stranger throw some large, brown paper bags into a nearby neighbor's trash cans. That was odd? I always believed I lived in a very safe neighborhood, so this was concerning. When I arrived at my front steps, I checked all around to make sure no one else was there before proceeding inside. I stopped short when I heard some faint whimpers coming from a red hibiscus bush to the right of the stairway. I brushed the branches aside and to my absolute surprise saw a tiny puppy standing next to two large, brown, paper grocery bags like the ones that stranger threw away. One other bag rested on its side and appeared as if the puppy had just crawled out of it. I looked at this most adorable creature and wondered how anyone could abandon something so precious.

I picked up the small dog and saw he was a boy, still noticeably young, but why the other two grocery bags? I held him and he nuzzled against my chest before I pulled both bags out from the bushes. I saw a note taped to one. "Please take the best care of him and give him a loving home. His name is Nicco, and all his belongings are inside these bags."

I looked at this helpless little creature and sensed he felt as lost in life as I did. At this moment, we needed each other so I decided to take him and his belongings inside to take care of him and keep him safe.

I was so distraught I couldn't eat dinner or watch TV but gave my new friend a saucer of water and some of the dry dog food I found in his bag. As I watched him eat, I spoke to him telling him everything was going to be all right. "You're so handsome and sweet, you need a name to match so I'm going to call you Nicky and give you a wonderful new home here with me."

I took Nicky into my bedroom, and I made him a bed using one of my extra bed pillows. I held him and hugged him. He whimpered as I placed him on his new bed but fell asleep right away.

For a brief time, Nicky distracted me from worry about

Marco, but it did not take long for my thoughts of despair to turn into anger. I was angry at him. Why did he leave without saying goodbye? I was angry at myself for falling in love with him. I took off that beautiful engagement ring he gave me and threw it in the wastepaper basket next to my nightstand, lay down on my bed fully clothed, and cried. I missed him and wanted him to return. What good is that engagement ring if I'd never see him again? My crying woke Nicky, who whimpered so loud, I had to pick him up and hug him.

Nicky and I both settled down again but for some peculiar reason, I awoke in the middle of the night thinking about Marco. This time I remained silent hoping not to wake my puppy. Considering all the fear and worry Marco gave me, I wondered why I should even care about him. My feelings made no sense. Before he left, he said he had to Travel back to several hours before his impending attack and needed my pendant, the key, for its aura of protection to defeat the two people who had killed him before and claim the treasure. Suddenly, I became drowsy and drifted off into a deep sleep, one where I found myself floating as light as a cloud and as transparent as a ghost over Marco's palazzo and from where I could view his journey.

Since I was sure I was invisible, I hovered directly over him and watched him go to his room unnoticed by his staff. He took that same hourglass he showed me in the park out of his pocket, placed it on his desk, and whispered to himself. "This will tell me how much time I have left before they try to kill me again."

As those tiny grains of sand fell from the top glass to the bottom, he removed that beautiful, carved wooden box from under the floorboards near his bed. Holding onto the box with both hands, he whispered: "Lana, love of my life, you and your key give me hope that I'll keep my promise to my grandfather and that our love will last for the rest of our lives. If your key unlocks this box, I'll know I possess the powers of your pendant to defeat my enemies and return to you as my true human self."

Marco carried the box to his desk. He removed my pendant from his pocket and placed it into the box's keyhole. As the key turned in the lock, Marco's face lit up. "It worked! It worked." He whispered amazed at his own achievement. He plopped down in his desk chair and lifted the box's lid with the utmost care to remove the crown wrapped in dense black netting. Placing the box aside, he focused on its contents. "Grandfather's stories were true. This is the most beautiful crown I have ever seen." I watched his fingers touch the intricate designs of the two ancient priests hammered in platinum between the crown's gold rims.

Opening his desk drawer, he removed a large magnifying glass to study the detailed etching. "I wish I had more time to do this. The intricate workmanship is magnificent. This crown serves as my inheritance, my promise kept." He stopped when sudden noises emanated from the downstairs hallway. "My murderers must be heading my way."

Marco put the magnifier down and whispered aloud. "Footsteps. Those loud footsteps approach just like before. This time I know what to expect and can prepare for my victory."

I watched as he remained silent for a few seconds to listen. Marco muttered, "They're making their way to the top of the marble steps to try to kill me again for my family's treasure."

He looked at his hourglass. "I have but mere minutes before the precise time of my past murder repeats itself. I must get ready."

He hurried and placed the crown back in the box, locked it, and stashed the box and the key under the bed pulling the bed skirt lower to cover them.

Overcome with worry, I thought. *Not the best hiding place, Marco, but I know you have little time to do anything else.*

Marco then grabbed his fencing gear, a face mask, and his vest, and struggled to put them on with the utmost speed before he raced to the wall over his desk and pulled down a large, very lethal-looking sword. He smiled as he juggled it in his arms. "Father's sword was always so much heavier than mine. Maybe if I had the time to get this the first time, they might not have killed me."

His timing was impeccable. Just as he turned to look at the doorway, it exploded open. Two masked intruders burst in with their swords drawn. As they made their way to Marco, the shorter one spoke in a high-pitched tone. "We're here to claim the treasure as our own."

Marco thought aloud. "I paid little attention to that voice the first time. It's high-pitched, like that of a woman. Why didn't I hear that before? Since the intruders are the same, I'll have to unlock some of their secrets to save my life."

I watched Marco study the shorter intruder for a few seconds before speaking directly to her. "I see by your stance that you are indeed a woman. Since you are standing in an attack position and point your sword directly at me, I must be on guard."

Positioned to lunge forward, the woman replied. "That priceless treasure will be ours after we kill you. Don't try to fight. It's hopeless. You will only make your death more painful. Give us the treasure, and we'll spare your life. A fair trade since that treasure will make us rich enough to live a life of royalty like yours."

My heart pounded as I watched the shorter intruder laugh while she directed her sword at Marco's heart the entire time she spoke. I gasped as the taller, more muscular intruder moved around the room waving his sword in the air trying to distract Marco before lunging in his direction. He cornered Marco against the nightstand near the right side of the bed.

By this time, the pair of thieves remained too close for comfort on either side of him. Marco took a quick lunge at the shorter one, making her back off. The tall intruder moved in closer to Marco prepared to strike. Marco nicked his right arm.

The intruder screamed. "Your stab will not daunt my efforts to get that key." He screamed in pain and held his arm as his wound bled out, causing them both to pause. Their pause gave Marco enough time to escape the taller one's next near fatal attempt on him by leaping on his bed right over the spot where he hid the box. I sensed that Marco was a skilled swordsman and realized he needed the best viewpoint to fend off two assailants at the same time. He pointed his sword at the taller one's heart and spoke. "The only way you'll get the key, my friend, is to kill me."

A duel ensued between the two of them. I watched Marco fight and worried about his chances of survival, but as before, he proved to be an expert swordsman. He may have been able to defeat one of them last time but the two attacking together made his imminent victory nearly appear impossible. But this time, I knew he had two big advantages on his side. He knew what to expect and possessed my pendant's aura of protection.

The shorter one tried her hardest to distract Marco by thrusting her sword back and forth at him. Marco remained focused, switching his body position as well as his sword between the two intruders. Frustrated, he yelled out. "Grandfather, protect me. I am defending our family's honor."

The taller one sneered as he continued to engage in the duel. "Your grandfather's dead. There's no way he can help you."

The loud clanging of their metal swords became deafening to my ears as the noise reverberated off the walls of that small third floor room. The tall assailant ordered his partner. "Attack him. I shall as well. He can't take on both of us at the same time. I'll hold him at bay while you stab him through his heart as deep as you can."

Marco looked determined and did not appear ready to give up. He whispered. "My thoughts of you, Lana, and our future together keep me strong for what I must do next."

His newfound energy helped him fight off the shorter one. She jumped on the bed to Marco's left while the taller one remained on the floor and approached from his right. Marco's sword shifted direction with each imminent threat. That challenge lasted ten minutes or so before the woman lost her footing, fell, and slipped onto the tile floor. She hit her head and appeared to have trouble getting up. Marco took advantage of her mishap, which distracted her partner, and pierced his left shoulder. He fell to the ground bleeding and in agony. Marco then jumped off the bed and stabbed him in his heart. The woman remained slow to get up and continue her assault on Marco. As his one attacker lay dying, he looked into Marco's eyes.

"Marco, forgive me. I don't understand how greed could have brought me to this moment. We used to be brothers."

The assailant gasped his last breath and died. Marco appeared shocked. "I recognize that deep voice. It sounded like Rinaldo, my friend since childhood, but how can that be? Why all the hatred? I have always treated him like family." Marco removed the mask from the dead assailant while the other attacker, still shaken, slowly tried to get back on her feet. Marco's eyes teared, displaying a deep sadness. "Rinaldo, why?"

The woman at last able to stand gasped. "Murderer! You murdered my lover! It will be my highest honor to kill you."

Marco remained vigilant as the shorter attacker continued to fight him with all her strength. "I am determined more than ever to kill you." She said as she lunged at Marco stabbing her sword deep into his right shoulder. Blood poured down his arm as he screamed in pain, but a look of determination filled Marco's eyes. He told his assailant. "I will defeat you not just for the treasure but for Lana, who gave me a reason to fight, to live, and to be able to love again."

Marco stared at the one intruder left to defeat him. She

snarled at him before ripping off her mask. "You have the right to know who is about to kill you."

The angry woman threw her mask on the floor. Marco's eyes grew wide in bewilderment as he gasped shocked to see that this woman was his own trusted servant, Sofia. His eyes filled with tears as he asked. "Sophia, why have you betrayed me? Haven't I always been good to you?"

She scoffed at him. I saw her hate for him ooze out from her eyes. "Why? Because I'm tired of your commands and have resented you from the first day I came to work for you. My hate grew more intense with each passing day. I should be the one wearing that pendant. I never told you about my royal bloodline, otherwise you would not have hired me.

"Imagine how different my life would be now if I possessed that treasure. I lost my chance to inherit the key by a mere twenty-one minutes. My grandmother, the Countess Lucia, and Lana's distant relative and great grandmother many times over, the Countess Gianna, were identical twins. Their mother possessed the pendant and following the strict rules of inheritance bequeathed it to Countess Gianna, who was the oldest twin by a mere twenty-one minutes.

"On the day your grandfather died, I waited behind his bedroom door and positioned myself so I could hear your conversation. I overheard your grandfather tell you about the crown, how it's worth a fortune, and if you find it, how you and your heirs will continue to live like royalty for the rest of your lives.

"I tried on more than one occasion to seduce you especially after I found out you were in pursuit of the pendant. You brushed me aside like I was joking. You know I am just as beautiful as Lana and just as smart, or you would not have trusted me with your foreign clients.

"I hated Lana not just because she had your love but because she wore the pendant that should have been mine, never willing to take it off even for a bath. Just the sight of her made me grind my teeth trying not to show my disdain for her. I had to be nice all the while hoping to gain her trust, catch her off guard, and steal her pendant. I was never disgusted by her skirt length but by the fact that she had your love and the key. They both should have been mine. It will be my highest honor to kill you since you murdered my Rinaldo. After I stab you to death, my wizard will send me to the future to kill your Lady Lana and take back my pendant. There will be nothing you can do about it.

"Today, you have stoked my fire of hate for you by killing my poor Rinaldo, my lover, my friend. We were to be married. I have had my future taken from me twice, the first losing the rights to that pendant and the second losing Rinaldo. Since you have taken away my future with Rinaldo, I now will kill you and take your precious future away from you.

"I have always resented your title especially since I lost my claim to one after the sudden death of my mother who had her title and all her wealth stripped by my stepfather, an unscrupulous count, a scoundrel who only wanted to marry her to obtain both. He forced me to leave the village. Like Rinaldo, I had no dowry or royal wealth. After my long absence from this village, many locals including yourself did not remember me. That's why it was so easy to gain your trust as a servant.

"There were many times when I worked for you, I tried to seduce you, but you would not have it. I wanted you to fall in love with me and not Lana. I resented Lana every time I saw her wearing my pendant. Rinaldo and I conspired to find a way to get even. If we killed you both, the key and the crown would be ours. This was our way of making up for what society took from each of us.

"Ha. You had no idea I was a skilled swordsman when you hired me. I only hope you will feel my wrath, my hatred for you as I keep stabbing you until you take your last breath. Your death will avenge my lover's murder and atone for my poverty and servant life. The treasure will then be all mine. Obtaining that treasured crown would have acquired royal titles for Rinaldo and me. He no longer had to be known as the son of a former Doge, but as a count in his own right and after we married, I would become his countess. Since you have taken him from me and that from us, take this."

A look of shock crossed Marco's face. I wondered if Sofia's surprise confession would impede his fighting ability. Marco knew it wasn't just the crown at stake. That's why he picked this day to return and defeat those two murderers, so he could step out of his shadow and begin life anew as a human being.

By Marco's determination, I sensed he was an adept enough competitor not to let his feelings interfere with this duel or he would die again, this next time, forever.

Sofia lunged once more at Marco with all the skill of an expert swordsman. Marco looked at her. "My dear Sofia, take this one for Lana." He jumped back, ready to lunge using his one uninjured arm. They fought until Marco seized upon an opening when Sophia turned for a few seconds to look at Rinaldo's lifeless body. He jumped forward and nicked Sofia's shoulder, making them equal combatants. Sofia, bleeding, positioned her sword for a kill shot but Marco kept changing directions to avoid contact. She raised her sword to take one strong stab at his heart, but he danced in and out of her sword's way, thus confusing her and creating an opportunity for him to put his blade straight through her heart. She held onto her wounded chest to stop the bleeding, but the bleeding was too profuse. It took only minutes for her to weaken and fall dead on the floor next to Rinaldo.

Marco ripped a sheet off the bed and wrapped it around his shoulder to stop his own intense bleeding. He sat on the edge of his bed and applied as much pressure as he could to his wound. He looked up to heaven and spoke. "Grandfather, I'm happy I kept my promise to you. I now can look forward to my future with Lana. However, the fact I had to kill my best friend and trusted servant saddens me. They had so much to live for, and I would have helped them any way I could. It pains me that they let greed and envy control their lives instead of love."

Marco remained on the bed holding his head and looking at the two people he had just killed. "I'm perplexed still trying to understand why you hated me enough to kill me, even more so that I had to kill you both to save my own life.

"Why would you turn against me? I always gave my friends and servants everything they asked of me." He looked at the two bodies. "Sofia, I never realized how much you hated me. And my best friend Rinaldo, when we were young, we were like brothers and shared everything. Since you both betrayed me, I should be happy you're dead, but instead I'm a broken-hearted man who had to kill the two people I trusted most because of your betrayal."

After a few moments, Marco looked at the sheet covering his wound. It was bright red, saturated with his own blood. "I need help." He stood, rushed over to the servant bell, and rang it repeatedly. When the staff heard repeated rings, they knew that to be a sign of trouble. In no time, I watched his two male servants, Otto and Eduardo, dash up the three flights of stairs to push open his bedroom door.

They stopped short at the threshold shocked to see Sofia dead, dressed like a man in black, and holding a sword. Her lover Rinaldo unmasked lay dead beside her with his sword at his side. As they entered, the rest of the servants slowly gathered and crowded in the small doorway to see if Marco was all right and stared stunned at the two bodies of their friends.

Eduardo questioned Marco first. "My Count, are you all right? What happened here? We heard the loud clanging of swords, but the noise was no more piercing than one of your regular practice sessions with our fencing master Joseph. We thought this might be an unscheduled one and decided not to come and interrupt. You should have rung the bell. We would have responded immediately. Now, you're bleeding so much we must assist to your wound at once."

Otto raced to the next room and returned with a small bucket of clean water and rags to wash Marco's wound along with enough bandages to wrap it. As he did, Eduardo advised the others gathered, "Otto will help our count while I will go notify the local authorities about the event and ask for help in removing the bodies."

Eduardo was not gone long, perhaps thirty minutes. When he returned, he informed everyone what would take place next. "Our local authorities said they will interview our count as soon as possible to verify his accounting of the event. They also advised me they would inform The Doge about the incident as well as Rinaldo's family about his death. Sofia, being a servant with no known family to date, will be buried in the public cemetery with assistance from the Republic. They are sending two wagons with attendants to assist with the removal of both bodies."

Eduardo slowly approached Marco. "Even with all my news, those of us gathered here need an explanation from you, my Count, as to what happened."

Marco nodded. "Of course I understand. Sofia worked here and Rinaldo visited us often. Many of us considered them our friends but after they fell in love and decided to marry, they teamed up out of resentment to kill me and steal my inheritance. Sofia told me during the duel that she wanted to live the royal life both of them felt had been taken from them. I had to kill them to save my own life and insure my future. Once all the facts become known, I hope The Doge will forgive me and clear my name since their actions were deceitful and murderous while mine were in self-defense."

Marco breathed a deep sigh of relief. "I was fortunate to

have survived this attempt on my life. In defending my honor, I kept my promise to my grandfather; but will that alone be enough for Othero to help me return to Lady Lana? I must send Lana a message. Otto when you have finished cleaning my wound, please summon Othero to come here at once. Tell him it's urgent."

CHAPTER
TEN

That night after what I had just witnessed, I couldn't sleep. I tossed and turned plagued by the visions I saw while floating in my trance-like state over Marco's duel. Some were good but most were terrifying, making me remember how worried I was for Marco's safety.

Without him in my life, I felt as abandoned as Nicky standing alone in that bush. I still loved Marco with all my heart. Even though my subconscious knew he had succeeded, I still wondered if I'd ever see him again and if he would keep his promise that we would be together again in the flesh.

The next morning, my mind was still filled with the vivid thoughts of his duel and of unlocking his family's treasure. Since I had received no message nor any sign from him, I realized I had to start my life over without him. Nicky sat next to my bed on the floor looking up at me and whimpering for attention. I picked him up and took care of his morning needs. Since I hated to leave him alone, my kind, elderly neighbor who watched me carry him inside offered to care for him while I was at work.

I walked to the library no longer hoping to see Marco's shadow. The shadow with whom I fell in love was gone from my life and had taken both the bad and the good with him. I remained angry because I felt betrayed. My mind still beat myself up for falling in love with him while trusting that his love had nothing to do with his obtaining my pendant.

I survived my workday with a sense of calmness I hadn't felt since before my parents' accident. Once back at home, I carefully stored those extra-heavy volumes on Venice under my coffee table. Never wanting to open them again, I thought about whether I should donate them to the library but concluded a charity auction would be better because that way I would be sure never to see them again.

My calmness extended to bedtime. That entire day, I felt like my worries were behind me. I had someone new in my life to love and caring for Nicky kept me calm. That night, I fell into a deep serene sleep. Good thing it was Friday night, because I overslept the next morning and would never have opened the library on time. If Nicky hadn't woken me up with his loud barking because he was hungry, I would have slept through the entire day.

I had no bad dreams about a shadow, murderers, or Time Travel. It was my most peaceful night in weeks. I believed my tranquility came from the fact that I was determined to remove Marco and all his baggage from my life. The shadow, my doubts about his love, Time Travel, all would now become part of my past.

My pendant, my family heirloom, was gone and all I had left was a very shaky promise of its return. To find my inner peace, I accepted and forgave my mistake of trusting him because I loved him with all my heart. With those thoughts swirling in my mind, I woke up happy to see the mid-morning sun burst through my window shades, happy to start my life anew and to share it with my beautiful puppy. I sat up in bed when suddenly the left side of my face itched. I hoped I wasn't allergic to Nicky but as I rubbed my cheek with my left hand, I felt something cool like a piece of metal and glass press against my face. I looked at my hand. *A ring?* I was surprised to see that same diamond and sapphire ring I had thrown in the trash now rested on my left-hand ring finger.

How could that happen? Did I sleepwalk? Even if I had, how and when did I retrieve it from my waste basket? Is my mind playing tricks or could the ring be Marco sending me a sign that he is coming back to me? Just the thought of that man made me both happy and angry at the same time. I yelled loud enough, I hoped, for him to hear wherever he was in the cosmos.

"Marco, if you can hear me, I demand to see you. I want to tell you in person how much I despise you. You broke my heart. You took something very precious from me, my love. After I get to tell you how I feel, I never want to see you or hear your name ever again. Do not contact me and don't have that silly little shadow of yours follow me ever again either."

I was so upset, I cried, meaning every word of it. When I finished my rant, I sat on the edge of my bed weeping. I picked Nicky up and hugged him for comfort but stopped when suddenly, I heard unusual noises coming from the front room. I looked over to see my bedroom door was partly open. Nicky scampered off my lap and out the partially open door. I became frantic, worried about my puppy, and afraid an intruder had broken in. I got up, picked up my small bedside lamp, and aimed it at the door ready to throw at any prowler.

I shuddered as those unusual noises that now sounded like footsteps approaching my bedroom door. I feared for Nicky, hoping he was safe and hiding under a table. When the door opened all the way, I had my lamp in hand and aimed it in that direction but couldn't throw it. I had to blink several times to make sure I wasn't looking at a mirage. Marco stood in my bedroom doorway. With one of his arms bandaged from the duel, he held Nicky in his other arm and smiled. "I see you received both my signs. I am holding the first one...a sign that I will always love you."

Was Nicky his sign? That's right. How could I forget? Marchesa had a dog named Nicco. That was very clever of him and very stupid of me not to connect the dots.

"I did but how did he arrive at my doorstep? Did that hooded stranger leave him for me?"

"Yes, she did. That hooded stranger was Aurellia, and I asked her to leave Nicco in case something happened to me. You would always have his love just like you have mine. I see you are once again wearing my second sign, our engagement ring, one that guaranteed my return to you and our impending marriage."

I gasped. "I felt so sorry for myself when you didn't return, I blocked my ability to see things clearly and look for your attempts to contact me. I still don't understand why I'm so happy to see you after what I just yelled out, but I am. Marco, I still love you with all my heart." He winked and with his free hand, held up my pendant.

"Lana, you're my lucky charm. With this key, I opened my grandfather's treasure, and its aura gave me the luck I needed to defeat the intruders who had murdered me in the past. I killed them both before they could kill me again and take our family's treasure. I am sad to tell you this, but Rinaldo and Sophia were the burglars who wished me dead."

My voice wavered still reflecting my surprise at his sudden appearance. "Rinaldo? Sophia? I don't understand how but because of my trance-like state last night, I already knew."

Stunned by the news, I asked, "Is that why Rinaldo came to the library looking for you? Why would they want to kill you?"

Marco walked over with Nicky in his arms, sat next to me on the bed, and held both of us close as he explained. "Rinaldo wanted a title of his own as well as enough money to live like a royal. My family's treasure would have allowed that. He no longer wanted to be known as the former Doge's son but wanted his old lifestyle back. Sofia wanted to live the life of royalty as well. She lost her royal title and wanted it back. She felt overlooked and resentful when she did not inherit your pendant. I think she coveted both more than anything else in her life. Rinaldo and Sofia fell in love but had more greed in their hearts than love. Right before I killed her, she told me she resented my wealth from the first day she came to work for me, even though I was good to her...to them both.

"I became depressed, sad that I had to kill them, but at the same time exuberant I survived, so I could come back to you, and we could be together. When we return to my time of 1588, my life, our life, will take a new course forward from that fatal day. I owe it all to the fact that I was your shadow, fell in love with you, and you trusted me with your pendant. The treasure is now ours for our future family. I left the wooden box and its contents safe in a marble vault under lock and key. When you called out my name, even in anger, Othero said he could hear your love shine through your rant. That love gave my life renewed hope and made it possible for my soul to return to my body and once again become the whole human being who is standing before you. Our love will no longer be in the shadows."

Marco placed Nicky on the bed between us, leaned over, and lifted my chain over my head with his good arm. He opened the clasp with both hands, put the pendant on it, and returned my pendant by gently dropping it over my head. He kissed my cheek.

"The second time around I had three things in my favor. The first was your love. I wanted to come back to you more than anything and marry you. The second was your pendant, the key, with its magical, protective aura along with your trust gave me the strength to persevere and keep my promise to my grandfather. And the third, the element of surprise was gone. I knew when they would come and that there would be two of them. Thoughts of our love got me through the toughest times of the attack."

Marco took my hand and kissed it. "My love, I want to marry you and for you to be my countess. I want us to be just like that happy couple in the book."

I looked down at my feet stunned to see that same volume through which we had Traveled suddenly appear like magic next to my bed and opened to that same page of The Doge's Ball with the illustration of the happy couple that so resembled us. I looked at Marco, "But how did this get here?" He winked. "Our love is magical. Wonderful things will happen because of that. We'll have a beautiful, royal Venetian wedding. Please say 'yes.' Your response will serve as Othero's energy to help us Travel."

He kneeled down. Nicky and I joined him on the floor. With my puppy by my side, I held both of Marco's hands. As I looked into his dreamy eyes, I knew our love was meant to be. Pendant or no pendant, Time Travel or not, I wanted to spend the rest of my life with him. I kissed his cheek. "Yes. Marco. Yes, I love you with all my heart and will marry you."

As tears of joy ran down my face, I glanced at that illustration and once again like the magic which happened before, the illustration disappeared, replaced by a big black hole.

My eyes met Marco's as he took my hand. I picked up Nicky, snuggled him in my other arm, while covering his eyes. I kissed the top of his head and held him as tight as I could. I knew it would break my heart to leave him behind.

This time our impending Travel did not frighten me perhaps because I knew what to expect or maybe because I was going back to marry the love of my life.

We looked down into that never-ending hole and leaned forward. Again, as we fell into it, the centuries passed us by like a fashion museum from the present back to Marco's time. This time, the fashions were of the most beautiful bridal fashions for brides and grooms.

Nicky whimpered all the way down even though I kept his eyes covered. The speed and motion of our descent through Time frightened him. As we approached our landing point, once again it appeared like we were going to crash, but having experienced this before, I knew we wouldn't. I smiled, held Marco's hand, and hugged Nicky taking my entire Travel in stride.

After we arrived, Marco's staff heard our happy chatter and assembled in the room adjacent to the balcony to welcome us with bouquets of flowers and cheers. We heard 'bravo' before they all came out to the balcony to hug us and wish us well. With Sofia no longer part of Marco's staff, Alana, one of his other servants, had assumed her position. She walked over, took my one free hand, and helped me stand. "Count Marcello and Lady Lana we are all so happy for you. Othero informed us of your engagement before you arrived. We all await your wedding plans with the hopes of making your special day the best day of your life."

Alana took one look at Nicky and laughed. "I see we have a new resident in the palazzo...a beautiful puppy who will be the most spoiled pet in all of Venice. I will take care of this little angel for you until you are settled."

Nicky barked as Alana approached him, gently took him from my arms, and stroked his fur, calming him down. As she did, I told her. "His name is Nicky."

Marco stayed busy hugging as many of his loyal staff as he could. He thanked them. "You are the most wonderful friends any man could have."

After their happy welcome, we followed them inside. Eduardo announced. "Please come with us into the dining room. We have a surprise for you. An engagement luncheon for all of us to share and celebrate your future together."

We walked into the dining room to see the long marble table loaded with roasted vegetables, pasta, sliced meats, and every imaginable dessert. We all ate, laughed, and drank wine until the sun set.

Exhausted from Travel, we left the party with Nicky earlier than Marco's staff. We stopped to wave from the doorway when Marco announced, "Thank you for your welcome, our beautiful luncheon, and for staying loyal to my family and our history.

"I want our wedding to be the most beautiful one Venice has ever seen but, most importantly, Lana and I want to invite all of you as our special guests. You will wear beautiful clothes and enjoy the wedding feast sporting the happiest faces in Venice. I will hire another count's staff for that day so you can celebrate with us." Excited, they cheered Marco's invitation.

Our wedding was as glamorous as any royal wedding could be. I wore a white satin gown with a beaded bodice trimmed with Venetian lace. My gown took my own breath away with its cathedral length train and veil. Marco looked as handsome as ever in his royal blue military uniform. We rode to the main cathedral in a gold gondola decorated with fresh flowers and ribbons and were married by Marco's longtime friend Roberto, now the Bishop of Venice, in a church filled with colorful flowers and happy attendees.

The most opulent wedding feast and party followed the ceremony in the main ballroom of the palazzo. Nicky looked so cute in his small, bejeweled collar and leash. Alana's young daughter had fun with him at the reception. Guests from all over the Venetian Republic attended in their fanciest attire and gorgeous jewels. Aurellia sent her greetings to us and to my surprise asked Othero to send my friend Sara to enjoy the festivities. Sara wore the loveliest peach gown and when asked, told me she enjoyed the adventure of her Time Travel. That's just like my Sara. As the band played, guests danced well into the night while wedding gifts piled as high as the ceiling in the main sitting room.

But when I think of our wedding day with all its opulence and beauty, my best gift was and still is Marco's love.

———

My mind snapped back to the present and my library presentation.

"Thank you for coming this afternoon. I can't believe it's been two years since I left my position here at the Naples Public Library. As you can see a lot has happened since then." My audience laughed when I rubbed my ever- growing belly filled with our first-born child and smiled at the standing room only crowd in the library's large conference room.

"I see so many familiar faces, those of co-workers, library patrons, and neighbors but am always delighted to discover some new ones as well. I'd like to reveal a bit of what happened to me during my absence but if you want to know the entire story, it's all here in my new book."

I held up one of the hard cover copies from the table in front of me waiting for my signature. "As you can see by the title 'Love in the Shadows' and the cover, the book describes a very steamy love story governed by time and threatened by conflict."

I stopped when I heard some hushed oohs from two older women in the back of the room both of whom I remember checked out explicit romances.

"Those of you who knew me as a librarian and historian like Mrs. Dufrene here in the front row, understood I never believed in Time Travel. It was always a far-fetched fantasy to me. That is, before I experienced it firsthand.

"I know that my perception of time is not an ordinary one. I'm sure one most of you will find it difficult to accept. But please believe me, what happened to me is not fiction. It's all true.

"'Love in the Shadows' does have a romance at its core, but the success of that romance depends upon the safe retrieval of a missing treasure from the twelfth century, important for its historical significance as well as its immeasurable value to the art world.

"Even with all the forementioned intrigue, my story began when I worked here as your librarian in the history section. My name then was Lana Brighton. I was neither a royal, nor married. All that was to come later, after the most exhilarating, daring, yet romantic adventure of my life.

"Two years ago, my life wasn't always this full and happy. I was a wall flower, much too shy to meet a man, especially the right one, and very afraid of falling in love. I never thought I could afford to travel on my salary, let alone to Venice, Italy, the home of my ancestors."

I grasped the beautiful antique pendant I wore around my neck and held it up for the audience to see. "This lovely but unusual garnet and diamond pendant has been in my family for hundreds of years, passed down to the eldest daughter of each generation. I discovered that it, too, unlocks a story hundreds of years old, mysterious, and worthy of history's attention."

Another woman in the front row I recognized, Mrs. Dinter, sighed. "Lana it's gorgeous. I remember you wearing that in the library, but I had no idea of its significance."

"Thank you." I paused to pull out a small oil painting from my purple brocade carry bag. "I'd like to pass this painting around the room to give you a tiny glimpse into my new life. This handsome, dashing man, five hundred and fifty years my senior, was and still is the man of my dreams. A hero, he risked his own life so we could stay together. At first, he appeared to me as a shadowy vision in the blink of my eyes but later when I learned that he was indeed real, it did not take long for our love to blossom. I love him with all my heart and most importantly, he loves me for me. His furry companion beside him is Nicky, our beautiful and beloved dog." I handed the small painting to an audience member in the front row to pass along to the others.

As the painting passed through the first row of attendees, I noticed the bent heads of those in the second row anxious to get their first glimpse. As the late afternoon sun began to form shadows on the bookshelves behind me, I heard continuous loud whispers from the audience until a hand shot up in the first row. An older woman with graying hair and kind eyes looked directly into mine.

"Lana, my name is Amelia Stone, and I'd like to thank you for all the help you gave me in the past. But I wonder, didn't Time Travel frighten you? My goodness, there are days I don't dare go to the grocery store because of all our local traffic or afternoon storms."

I shot her a kind smile. "Thank you for your question. Of course, the first time we Travelled, I was frightened out of my mind. But remember I was with the love of my life who helped me get through this and much more as you'll read in my book. I guess finding the love of your life can change your entire perspective. Marco changed mine. My love for him is as strong today as the day we fell in love."

Amelia nodded and sat down as another hand from the row behind her appeared. A younger woman who appeared to be in her late teens or early twenties stood eager to ask her question.

"Hi Lana, my name is Charity White, and I started to frequent this section of the library after you left. I would love to Time Travel because I love history and would be able to watch it as it happens besides meeting some of my ancestors who I've done extensive research on. Tell me, is NASA or some other space or scientific agency hoping to make this possible for us mere mortals? I would volunteer if asked. Yikes just the thought of it makes me excited."

"Charity, thank you for your question, but I know of no such study at the present. Who knows what the future may bring? Remember, Time Travel occurs only for a compelling cause that needs to connect the present with the past or vice versa. It is a supernatural feat since a wizard must initiate Travel through a special spell to help resolve that issue."

Charity nodded and sat back down as I began to wrap up my talk.

"I'd like to thank you again for attending my book signing. As you can see, I have plenty of books to sign. If you'd like to purchase one, please form a line to the right of the table and Michelle from my publisher's office will accept your payment and take instructions as to how you would like me to sign your book. Before you do, please enjoy a small cup of cider that's being handed out and join me in a traditional Italian toast, Cent' Anni. May you live for one hundred years! Thank you again!"

As I signed my new name to each copy, The Contessa Lana Banelli, I beamed, grateful for my new life filled with Marco's love and looking forward to the birth of our first child, ever so happy I had worked in this library and that his shadow chose to follow me.

ACKNOWLEDGMENTS

I would like to thank my fellow author Sarah Stanton Andre for her encouragement and wisdom.

THANK YOU FOR READING

———

Did you enjoy this book?

We invite you to leave a review at your favorite book site, such as Goodreads, Amazon, Barnes & Noble, etc.

DID YOU KNOW THAT LEAVING A REVIEW...

- Helps other readers find books they may enjoy.
- Gives you a chance to let your voice be heard.
- Gives authors recognition for their hard work.
- Doesn't have to be long. A sentence or two about why you liked the book will do.

ABOUT THE AUTHOR

Mariah Lynne takes her readers along on exciting adventures. Meet memorable characters as you outsmart present day murderers, Time Travel to catch a thief stealing a duchess' necklace or be rescued by a handsome knight; perhaps fall in love all over again through romances that make you smile and melt your heart. Her heroines are fearless, strong-willed independent women who will entertain and inspire you.

A resident of a beautiful Florida Gulf Coast barrier island for more than thirty years, she loves to weave the local color of islanders who come from all over the world to live there into her characters as well as set her stories in the scenic island backdrop that serves as her backyard. An animal lover, all her heroines have pets. Her books include: The Love Gypsy, Shadows Across Time, The Duchess' Necklace, A Gem of a Murder, Claws for Justice, Paws for Christmas, Max Canine Concierge of Love, A Christmas Wish for Love, The Jellybean Matchmaker, and Love in the Shadows.

Website: www.MariahLynne.com
E-mail: MariahLynneAuthor@yahoo.com

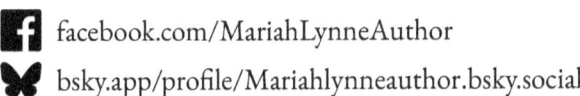

facebook.com/MariahLynneAuthor

bsky.app/profile/Mariahlynneauthor.bsky.social

ALSO BY MARIAH LYNNE
WITH SATIN ROMANCE